Lorelei Heard A Sudden Crash.

Horrified, she dashed down the steps, only to come to a screeching halt at the scene that met her eyes.

Lucas was picking himself up off the floor, or at least trying to. High above, near the ceiling, the door to one of the cabinets was swinging open.

"Are you hurt? What happened?"

"It's okay," Lucas said magnanimously. "I should've known better—the coffin should have taught me a lesson. I was up there, checking the ceiling, and the cabinet door swung open. Suddenly I found myself looking at a collection of severed heads. But, hey, that happens all the time. No sweat."

"They're from the movie *Dr. Guillotine*—"

"Oh, well, that explains it," Lucas said in a tone that suggested that it didn't really. He eyed her cautiously. "Any more little surprises I should know about?"

"Well—there are mementos scattered around the house. You shouldn't be shocked by anything you see...."

Dear Reader,

Happy summer reading from all of us at Silhouette Desire! I know you'll enjoy this July's selections as much as I do, starting with a scrumptious *Man of the Month,* Dan Blaylock, hero of Cait London's *Midnight Rider.* This book will send you running to the nearest ranch so you can find a man like this of your very own.

Robin Elliott fans—and there are plenty of you out there—will be thrilled to note that she's made a return to Silhouette Desire with the delightful, suspenseful *Sophie's Attic.* Welcome back, Robin!

And Jackie Merritt, whose heroes are often "back at the ranch," opts for a change of scenery... but no change of excitement... in *Shipwrecked!* Rounding out the month are three books that are simply not to be missed: *Flirting with Trouble* by Cathie Linz, *Princess McGee* by Maura Seger, and *An Unsuitable Man for the Job* by Elizabeth Bevarly. Don't let July go by without reading these books.

So, until next month, go wild with Desire—you'll be glad you did.

Lucia Macro

Senior Editor

MAURA SEGER

PRINCESS McGEE

SILHOUETTE *Desire*®

Published by Silhouette Books New York

America's Publisher of Contemporary Romance

SILHOUETTE BOOKS
300 East 42nd St., New York, N.Y. 10017

PRINCESS McGEE

Copyright © 1992 by Maura Seger

ISBN: 0-373-05723-7

First Silhouette Books printing July 1992

All the characters in this book have no existence
outside the imagination of the author and have
no relation whatsoever to anyone bearing the same
name or names. They are not even distantly
inspired by any individual known or unknown
to the author, and all incidents are pure invention.

Printed in the U.S.A.

MAURA SEGER

and her husband, Michael, met while they were both working for the same company. Married after a whirlwind courtship that might have been taken directly from a romance novel, Maura credits her husband's patient support and good humor for helping her fulfill the lifelong dream of being a writer.

Currently writing contemporaries for Silhouette Books and historicals for Harlequin Books and mainstream, she finds that writing each book is an adventure filled with fascinating people who never fail to surprise her.

Prologue

While they were in the church, the weather cleared. The damp fog of morning lifted and the sun broke through just as Lorelei McGee stepped out onto the steps in front of the glass-and-cedar structure. It was still cold, however, and she was glad of the coat Aunt Melinda had put around her shoulders.

Blinking in the sun, she watched as her father's casket was carried gently to the waiting hearse. Banks of flowers rested upon it. Friends gathered close, watching silently. Many were old, some needing wheelchairs, but they had all come to bid Vincent McGee a fond farewell.

Lorelei took a deep breath. The air smelled of the sea, never far away in this northern California town perched on a ridge high above the Pacific. San Cristobal was a small town made up of a few thousand residents, tucked high in the northernmost corner of the state between the Sisikou Mountains and the ocean.

It was a picturesque place that combined a lingering air of 1890s Victoriana with a leap ahead into the next century. The church itself was a postmodern masterpiece designed to blend into, rather than change, its surroundings. Indeed, when the light hit it correctly, the entire building almost seemed to vanish into the ancient pine forest. Yet less than half a mile away, the main street was lined with deep-porched, gingerbread fantasies painted in a riot of colors, festooned with hanging pots of geraniums and curtained in lace.

Vincent McGee had loved the contrast between old and new. In San Cristobal he had found his own refuge from the turbulent world. He had lived there for four decades, arriving several years before Lorelei's birth. She was infinitely glad that he had been able to end his days, peacefully and with dignity, in the place he loved so well.

Uncle Thad touched her elbow gently. She broke off her reverie and managed a faint smile. "Is everyone all right?" she asked.

He nodded. "Oh, yes, I think so. Rosalind is looking a bit piqued, but she'll hold up. It was a lovely service."

Lorelei agreed. The minister was a young man who hadn't known her father well. In his final years, Vincent had stayed largely to himself, seeing old friends but otherwise not venturing out much. Nonetheless, Reverend Burns had made a good job of it.

So, too, had the many friends who had stood to say a few words about the life of a man whose public face had been so different from his private nature.

"Sam almost had me in tears," Lorelei said as together they walked to the car.

Thad chuckled. "I know what you mean. I almost laughed myself sick when he started talking about the good ol' days back at Star Studios. Sweet Lord, the things we got into."

"I hadn't heard the one about Dad and the elephant," Lorelei said. The driver opened the back door and stood aside as she got into the car. Thad followed, a little slowly because of his arthritis. He would be eighty on his next birthday, three years

younger than Vincent had been, but his eyes still
shone as brilliantly as ever.

"How did you miss that one?" he asked as he took
his seat beside her. It had been agreed that Thad
would ride with her to the cemetery, along with only
a few of the others, who followed in their own cars.

The rest would return to the house. A buffet
luncheon would be served and there would be a
screening of one of Vincent's favorite movies, *Dr.
Doom*. Aunt Melinda was in charge of all that. Lorelei caught sight of her plump figure, swathed in
purple silk, climbing into one of the limousines.

"Melly's going to have her work cut out for her
with this crowd," Lorelei mused. She adored her
father's friends, but the fact was most of them came
from a generation that had worked hard and played
the same way.

Now in their seventies and eighties, they saw no
reason to change their habits. Sparkling water, white-
wine spritzers and pasta salads wouldn't do for this
bunch.

"How many cases of champagne did Dad order?" Lorelei asked.

"Enough," Thad assured her. "He loved planning parties and he knew this would be the last one
for him, so he did it up right. Don't worry. Everything will be fine."

"We'll run out of caviar."

"You're supposed to. If you have any left over, you'd think we were Philistines."

"If the beef is overdone, Pat and Pete will have a fit."

Pat and Pete were a pair of comedians who had gotten their start as kids in the old vaudeville days, gone over to radio and then hit it big on television in the 1950s. Their slapstick brand of humor had stayed hot up until the mid-sixties. The decline in their popularity had turned their attention to the California real estate market, in which they had made millions. Lately their movies were enjoying a revival. Rumored to hate each other and fight constantly, they still went everywhere and did everything together.

"They'll make the best of it," Thad assured her. "We all had far too much respect for Vincent not to give him a topflight send-off."

"I appreciate that," Lorelei said softly. "You were all Dad's family as much as me." She bit her lip as she looked out the car window. "I just wish I'd been here with him."

Thad squeezed her hand gently. "If he'd wanted it that way, you would have been. Vincent knew that. But he had a good end, sweetheart, on his own terms. There's a great deal to be said for that."

Lorelei supposed he was right. The love she and her father had shared was strong and solid. She missed him, but she really believed that he had gone on to something better.

"Have you thought about what you'll do with the house?" Thad asked as the car turned a corner and sped up slightly. The town was left behind as they headed for the cemetery.

"I'm keeping it," Lorelei said.

His thick white eyebrows rose. "Dear child, you aren't serious?"

She smiled wryly. "I'm afraid so."

"Have you taken a serious look around?"

"Not yet, there hasn't been time and, I admit, I haven't felt much like it. But it can't have changed too much in four years."

"Well, no, I suppose not. Vincent was a dear man, but that house...I'll never know what he was thinking of when he built it."

"Neither will I," Lorelei admitted, "but whatever the inspiration was, I love the result and I'll fight tooth and nail to keep it."

Thad cast her a sidelong look, the same one he'd used to such devastating effect on his leading ladies back in the thirties and forties. He'd known Lorelei all her life and took his responsibilities as her god-

PRINCESS McGEE   13

father seriously. Her decision to keep the house—or at least try to—worried him.

She looked so delicate sitting there, wrapped in Melly's old sable coat, which was much too big for her. Her mahogany hair framed her pale, heart-shaped face and was spread out over her shoulders, its darkness in direct contrast with the unusual lightness of her blue eyes, which had always reminded him of the water off Capri.

He had honeymooned there with his third—or was it fourth?—wife. No, Capri had been Penelope—he could still remember those toreador pants she'd worn—and she was definitely his third. Also his sixth, in that monumental folly of his old age, which had cost him no end. But never mind about that.

"Pen isn't going to be here, is she?" he asked.

Lorelei shook her head. "She and Aunt Melly can't stand each other."

"Melinda always was a shrewd judge of character," Thad said dryly.

Lorelei agreed, glad that her aunt was there to help. Melinda Taylor wasn't actually related to her, but she had been a constant presence throughout Lorelei's life, much as Thad had been.

"What originally caused the quarrel between her and Pen?" she asked.

"Melly beat her out for the part of Amber in *Light of Day,* remember?"

Lorelei didn't actually, since the hit movie had been an Oscar winner back in 1939, but she didn't say so. Thad was like the others, sometimes forgetting that she wasn't really one of them.

Now twenty-six, she had been born when Vincent McGee's career was at an ebb. He was living in comfortable retirement and had been delighted to suddenly have a baby daughter at a time when many of his contemporaries were satisfied with grandchildren.

She had grown up surrounded almost entirely by people who could have been her grandparents. Over the years, the differences in their ages hadn't seemed to count for much, but occasionally Lorelei wondered if she shouldn't have made more of an effort to get to know people closer to her in years.

She pushed the thought aside and looked out the window again. They had reached the cemetery on the bluffs overlooking the ocean. A soft smile touched her lips. Vincent had chosen well.

Thad helped her from the car. She drew the coat more closely around her and walked the short distance to the grave site. The others, a half dozen in all, were there already. They nodded comfortingly and made room for her.

Carefully, she glanced around. Everything was as she had asked, restrained and very private. A sigh of relief escaped her.

Thad heard her and nodded in understanding. Although Vincent McGee had left the American screen before many of today's moviegoers had even been born, he was still well enough remembered that the media would have turned out to cover his funeral—had they known the time and place of it. But more than even Vincent himself, they would have been drawn by Lorelei.

Thad shook his silvered head as he thought of that. The public was a fickle beast at best, but it had never lost its fascination with Vincent McGee's little girl—Princess McGee, as some columnist had dubbed her. The child's ethereal beauty had provided such a contrast to her father's reputation as the Master of Horror that the public had been entranced.

But just as the fascination with her had reached a peak, Lorelei had slipped from view. She had left them—as the showbiz adage went—wanting more. Much, much more.

The service proceeded. Lorelei held tight to Thad's hand as she bid her father godspeed on what he had always referred to as "the next stage of this marvelous journey."

Vincent McGee had retained a certain childlike innocence and enthusiasm to the very end. She couldn't help but think that somewhere out there he still did.

When the last prayer was said, she returned to the car with Thad. Her thoughts were on the just-concluded service and the luncheon ahead.

She therefore did not notice the sports car parked nearby, or the man seated in it. He was in his mid-thirties, casually if expensively dressed, with thick black hair that was slightly longer than the current fashioned dictated. It brushed the collar of his linen jacket. One blunt-tipped finger tapped impatiently against the steering wheel. His steel-gray eyes were narrowed and his features darkly brooding as he watched Vincent McGee being lowered into his final resting place.

One

————

Lucas Messina waited until the last of the limousines had left the cemetery before he departed. Earlier, he had paid his respects to the members of his family who were buried there.

He did this not because he was in any way a morbid man, on the contrary he loved life with unceasing strength and vigor. He did it because he had been raised to believe that it was right and proper to show respect for those who had gone before, to remember their struggles and accomplishments, and to draw wisdom and encouragement from them.

In this world of endless, shifting change and constant emphasis on the new, Lucas was an old-fashioned man. He made no apologies for it.

He was thoughtful as he maneuvered the 1936 Cord convertible back onto the main road. He had found the car eight years before, standing on cinder blocks, in a junkyard. Little more than a wrecked shell, something about it had challenged and inspired him.

He had rebuilt it from the ground up and liked the results far more than he would have if he'd just gone out and plunked down money for a status automobile. What he had, instead, was a piece of history that was also the tangible result of his own labor. That counted. In Lucas's book, a man should see the fruits of his work. To be denied them was to be cheated.

He reached the offices of Messina Construction a few minutes later and parked behind the building. Two years before, he'd moved the company to San Cristobal, but he'd spent most of that time on the road. It was only recently that he'd come even close to settling down, and that only tentatively.

Entering through a back door, he sprinted up the stairs to his top-floor office. The view from there was spectacular, looking out as it did toward the ocean. But Lucas barely noticed it. He accepted the sheaf of messages his secretary held out with one hand and with the other he undid the knot of his tie.

"Sal here yet?" he asked as he strode into his office. It was a spacious, airy room that was well furnished and comfortable, but not particularly luxurious. Besides two substantial worktables and a cluster of couches and chairs, the most notable feature was the state-of-the-art computer system, used for everything from logging E-mail to drawing complex plans.

"In the conference room," Lisa Bergen said as she followed him. "The quarterly report is on your desk and the price data you wanted is in the computer. Victor Cabot wants to know if you're free for lunch Monday." She consulted her notebook. "Personnel had candidates lined up for the engineering spot and they want a go-ahead to start booking appointments for you beginning the end of this week. I told them okay provisionally."

"That's fine," Lucas said as he took a quick look through his phone messages. None needed to be answered immediately. "Anything else?"

"Pete says they've hit one hundred percent at Laguna. The last closing was just scheduled this morning."

Lucas made a mental note to get back to the Laguna project manager. They'd sold out the vacation home complex three months sooner than expected and that in the midst of a housing market still described as slow.

"Nice work," he said. "Anything on Mountain Falls?"

"Jerry says they're getting more traffic there than anywhere else in the area and he should go past eighty percent this month."

Lucas nodded. Both the major Messina projects on the market were doing better than hoped. The stock analysts would be pleased, the investors would be happy, and his bankers would be lining up to lend him more money. Which was all well and good, but he wasn't about to rest on his laurels.

"I'll be in with Sal," he said as he headed back out of the office. "We ought to wrap up by midafternoon. I'll be leaving early."

Lisa looked startled. She couldn't remember the last time her boss had left the office before she did. He was usually there when she came in and she knew that he frequently worked at home on the weekends. So what made today different?

She would have liked to ask, but Lucas didn't encourage that kind of familiarity. Although he was unusually considerate of his employee's personal lives—providing parental leave and an on-site child care center that even had a special facility for kids who were sick—he kept his personal life to himself. Lisa could only speculate, which she did enjoyably for all of the three minutes it took her to get back to work.

Sal was Salvatore Frattori, Lucas's cousin and his main man on project development. With a graduate degree in architecture from Yale, Sal could have gone anywhere, but he preferred staying in the family business. He owned a nice piece of stock, which he added to regularly, drew a good salary and got the satisfaction of seeing his ideas become reality in a way that wouldn't have been possible elsewhere. All thanks to Lucas, who, the way Sal saw it, had some weird kind of genius for overcoming problems and making things happen.

"Let's see it," Lucas said as he walked into the conference room. The plans were already spread out on the table. He looked through them, one by one, nodding as he did so.

"Looks good," he said. "I like what you did with the roof lines."

"It's more interesting this way," Sal agreed. "I was surprised that the additional cost worked out to be so small."

"I figured it would be," Lucas said as he continued studying the plans. They were for the most ambitious project Messina Construction had undertaken yet, an entirely new town, intended for a coastal tract south of Seattle.

The look was modified Victorian—houses with gabled roofs, porches and cupolas on neighborhood-size streets, with schools, shops and businesses clustered nearby. There were also several office parks within easy walking distance that were already almost fully sold. The town was a hit before the first spadeful of dirt was turned on the first foundation. But several years of dogged preparation had gone into what only looked like an overnight success. Nobody knew that better than Lucas and Sal.

"You ought to take Maria away somewhere," Lucas said, "have a little celebration."

Sal grinned. "As it so happens, we were talking about that just the other day. She's got some idea we ought to have another baby."

"Four's a nice number."

"Easy for you to say, buddy. I don't see you lining up to change diapers and do 2:00 a.m. feedings."

Lucas shrugged. He was crazy about all his nieces and nephews, not to mention second and third cousins, but he had to admit there were times when he wondered why he didn't have any kids himself. Of course, it would have helped if he'd ever gotten around to getting married.

He'd been working since he was fourteen, and in the twenty years since then, he'd built a business plenty of men would have envied. He'd also had his share of relationships, but they'd always been on the sidelines of his life, never right at the heart of it. He didn't regret that, but he wasn't altogether comfortable with it, either.

"Use the cabin up at the lake if you want to," he suggested. "It's still cool this time of year, but it's real peaceful."

Sal looked interested. "I might take you up on that. But it wouldn't hurt you to get away for a while yourself. When was your last vacation?"

Lucas started to answer, realized he couldn't remember, and laughed. "I'll get around to it one of these days. First, there's something else I need to take care of."

"Oh, yeah? What?"

Lucas hesitated. But instead of answering immediately, he rolled up his shirtsleeves and sat down at the conference table. Sal took the chair next to him. The quick once-over was done; it was time for the final in-depth analysis of the plans.

In-depth meant just that—before he was done, Lucas would have reviewed every element going into the houses, from the specifications for plumbing and wiring to the exact design of the doorknobs. It would take the better part of the day, but when it was done everything would be in place to begin production and carry it through without interruptions or delays. That kind of relentless attention to detail was a big part of Messina Construction's success. Lucas knew what he wanted and he knew how to get it. Heaven help anyone who got in his way.

"Nothing much," he said finally, in answer to Sal's question. He glanced at his cousin. "Vincent McGee was buried today."

"Oh, yeah, I'd heard he died." A thought occurred to him. "Hey, was that where you went this morning?" At Lucas's nod, Sal whistled softly. "You don't ever forget, do you?"

"Should I?"

"It was a long time ago," his cousin said softly, "and God knows, the whole family's come a long way since. What's Vincent McGee got to do with anything anymore?"

"He doesn't," Lucas said. "But there's still the house."

"It's a pile of stone, that's all it is."

"No," Lucas said quietly, "it's much more. The Messinas poured everything into that house. We gave it our blood, literally. And Vincent McGee stole it from us. That kind of thing you don't forget."

"So what're you going to do about it?" Sal asked.

A faint smile lifted the corners of Lucas's mouth. He laughed softly. "What else? I'm gonna make them an offer they can't refuse."

Sal shot him a disbelieving look, but said nothing more. When Lucas got a certain look in his steel-gray eyes, nobody with any brains argued with him. That look was there now. It made Sal very glad that he wasn't on the receiving end. But it also made him just a bit suspicious.

"This, uh, doesn't have anything to do with McGee's daughter, does it?"

Lucas scowled. "What makes you ask that?"

Sal shrugged, already sorry he'd brought it up. "Nothing, I just remember when that Vogue cover came out, you were kind of struck by her. You know?"

"You're dreaming. This is business."

"Sure," Sal said hastily. "Whatever you say." But he couldn't shake the idea that he'd stumbled onto something. The look in Lucas's eyes did nothing to convince Sal that he shouldn't be just a bit concerned for Miss Lorelei McGee, no matter what her family had done to his.

In Sal's opinion, the house was ancient history. The same couldn't be said for the beautiful woman who undoubtedly had no idea what Lucas had in mind, whatever that might be. Only loyalty to his cousin kept Sal from feeling a twinge of compassion for her.

Lorelei sat down with a sigh of relief, eased her feet out of her shoes, and put her head back against the chair. It was two days later, and most of her father's friends had finished paying their respects and left. Only Thad and Melly were still there. They were seated, off by themselves, in a corner of the vast living room, probably rehashing past indiscretions, Lorelei thought with a smile.

She was very tired. The strain of her father's death and the funeral had taken its toll. There was a soft, bruised sadness in her. Although she accepted what had happened as part of the natural order of all things, she also knew that she would miss him. He had, above all, always been her friend.

She glanced around, noting the worn furniture, the faded brocade wallpaper and the faint air of disuse that hung over the room. By itself, it was a marvelous place, with a soaring ceiling, a fireplace straight out of a medieval castle and a sweeping perspective out over the ocean. But time and neglect had blurred the former elegance. Looking up, she could see a stain on the ornate plaster ceiling, where water had leaked through not long ago. There were other such places throughout the house, as well as much, much more.

But she wasn't going to think about that now. Her head hurt, her spirit was drained and she needed to rest.

She stood, caught Melly's eye, and said, "I'm going upstairs for a bit."

Her aunt nodded, her face creased with concern. "Get some sleep, dear. You need it."

"If anything comes up," Thad added, "we'll take care of it."

Lorelei smiled gratefully. Beyond the living room was a large entry hall dominated by a twin marble staircase with a heavy mahogany banister. As a child, Lorelei had liked nothing better than to slide down that banister at top speed, terrifying any servant unfortunate enough to catch her at it.

But the servants were long gone, the banister needed repairing and the pleasures of her childhood were no more than mere memories. She climbed the stairs slowly, only then realizing how truly exhausted she was. By the time she reached her room, she barely had the strength left to take off her clothes and tumble into the high four-poster.

Below, in the entry hall, the doorbell chimed. Thad was just pouring them both a brandy, so Melly went to answer it. She found herself looking at a tall, muscular man, darkly handsome but with something about him that sent a little shiver through her.

In the best *grande dame* manner that had served
her so well in her long career, Melly lifted her chin,
narrowed her eyes and said, "Yes?"

"I'd like to see Miss McGee," Lucas told her
pleasantly. To him she was an elderly woman, nicely
if a bit elaborately dressed, who reminded him a little of his Great-Aunt Lucia. Not for a moment did
he realize that he was looking at *the* Melinda Taylor,
former star of screen and stage, and heartthrob to
millions, and even if he had, the name wouldn't have
meant anything to him.

It would have to his grandfather, who, self-
possessed man that he had been, would still have felt
a rush of excitement at coming face-to-face with
what was once Hollywood's most glamorous leading lady. But that was then and this was now. Lucas
had no idea who Melly was nor did he particularly
care. His interest was solely Vincent McGee's
daughter and then only because she was a means to
an end.

Melly was a sensible woman when she chose to be,
but she had just spent several days basking in the at-
tentions of old friends and the abrupt return to reality did not suit her. She took an instant dislike to
the presumptuous young man, who seemed to have
no notion of whom he was speaking to. In her view,

that was the trouble with the present generation, they had no sense of history.

To be fair, Melly was also tired and more than a little melancholy over the passing of her friend. Seeing Thad again was also a strain. All in all, she was not at her best and she knew it.

Which was what prompted her to do what she always did under such circumstances, take refuge in one of her favorite roles. Reaching into the trunk of her copious memory, she plucked out a voice, an expression, a posture that she had used to such splendid effect as the Csarina Alexandra on Broadway during the 1931 season.

To the echoes of long-faded applause, she said, "Miss McGee is not at home."

Lucas stared at her, dumbfounded. Any resemblance to Great-Aunt Lucia was gone. In her place was a woman who looked haughty, self-contained and not a little contemptuous.

"You mean she went out?" he asked.

"I mean," Melly said succinctly, "that she is not at home." She made to shut the door.

Lucas held it open with one hand, ignoring her frosty scowl. "In that case, I'd like to leave a message."

"Of condolence, I presume," Aunt Melly/Csarina Alexandra said. Looking down her nose at him—

no mean feat considering that he towered over her—
she added, "Nothing else would be remotely acceptable."

Oh, it wouldn't, would it? Lucas thought. Who
was kidding who here? Lorelei McGee had left her
father's home four years before and, as far as he
knew, had never been back, not even when the old
man lay dying. That hardly argued for a close relationship.

Yet here was this old battle-ax trying to make him
feel like some lowlife for daring to address the high-
and-mighty miss.

Maybe that shouldn't have bothered him, but
standing there on Vincent McGee's doorstep, it
stung. A lot.

"Forget it," he said, and turned away, but not
before something caught his eye. The marquetry
floor of the hall needed polishing. The walls could
use some painting, too. His gaze narrowed. Now that
he thought of it, some of the flagstones in front of
the door were loose and there were weeds on the
lawn.

"Whom shall I say called?" Melly asked his back
as it belatedly occurred to her that she had been rude.

"Never mind," Lucas said over his shoulder. "I'll
be back." But not, he added silently, until the way
was clear, and then only to get a better idea of what

he was dealing with. Something had happened to the house that he hadn't been aware of. He was going to find out what that something was—and why—before he went any further.

Melly shut the door thoughtfully. Lorelei hadn't mentioned anyone coming by, so presumably he wasn't a friend of hers. Too bad, that, since he wasn't hard to look at. She smiled faintly. Truth was, if she was twenty—oh, all right, forty—years younger, she would have been considerably nicer to him. There had been a time...

"Everything all right?" Thad asked her as she returned to the living room. He held out a snifter of brandy.

Melly took it and let her smile deepen. She looked into the eyes of the man she had never married but had always meant to, and said, "Fine, darling. Everything's just fine."

She couldn't have been more wrong.

Two

———

Melly and Thad left together the next day. Lorelei wasn't precisely glad to see them go, but their departure did free her to get down to work. The House—which she had come to think of with a capital H—was top priority.

What was she going to do? She loved the old place, and the mere thought of parting with it made her hurt inside. But there was no getting around the truth. Vincent McGee's pride and joy was in danger of turning into a tumbledown wreck unless she got hold of the situation quickly.

To do that, she needed help. The problem was that she couldn't just leaf through the phone directory, find a likely plumber, plasterer, electrician, gardener, painter—and whatever else would be needed—and have them drop by. Her income as an illustrator was more than ample for her normal everyday needs, but not for this.

She needed someone who would work cheap and who had a variety of skills. In short, she needed that legendary creature of American myth—a handyman.

San Cristobal had a weekly newspaper that came out on Mondays. By dint of a little luck and a lot of arm-twisting, Lorelei got her ad in under the wire. It ran the next day.

Wanted. Skilled handyman to help resurrect beautiful but aging house. Small salary but much psychic compensation. Apply: McGee, 34 Pacific Cliffs Road

In most parts of the country, it wouldn't have stood a chance. But this was California and Lorelei figured she had at least a shot at getting help.

She was, therefore, not overly surprised when she opened the door early the following morning to find herself staring at a very large, very handsome man wearing work clothes and a smile.

"Hi," he said. "You the lady who placed the ad?"

For a fleeting instant, she wondered what ad he was talking about. With thick black hair, rugged features, piercing gray eyes and a build that didn't quit, he could have answered something from the personal column and thrilled any woman who got him. But the hammer hanging from his tool belt suggested he had other things in mind.

"Come on in," she said, her natural caution dented by the thought that here, within her grasp, so to speak, might be the answer to her problem.

"I'm Lorelei McGee," she said when the door had closed behind him. Mentally she braced herself for his response. Not too many years ago the name had been enough to raise eyebrows at the very least. But it didn't seem to mean anything to him.

"I'm Lucas Messina," he said, and held out his hand. Was it her imagination or did he, too, pause fractionally as if thinking his name might have some significance for her?

Beyond thinking it a nice name and well suited to the man, Lorelei had no other reaction. She took his hand, finding it warm, strong and callused, and returned his smile.

Never mind the little shiver of excitement that ran through her as their skin touched. She absolutely wasn't going to pay any attention to that.

Lucas let go of her hand, but continued to look at her steadily. His expression revealed nothing of his thoughts. Close up, she was even more beautiful than when he had seen her in the cemetery. Her mahogany hair was caught back in a bun at the nape of her neck, emphasizing the classic purity of her features. She wasn't wearing makeup, yet her cheeks were lightly flushed and her crystalline blue eyes were naturally framed by thick lashes. The cotton blouse and slacks she wore were simple to the extreme, yet they only served to emphasize the willowy perfection of her figure.

She was one of those rare women nature had chosen to lavish with an excess of grace and beauty, yet she seemed completely unaware of it. Her manner was relaxed and friendly, without any of the self-consciousness or vanity he'd expected.

He thought about what he knew of her—her early, tumultuous life in the spotlight and her sudden retreat into anonymity. His brows drew together as he tried to reconcile the seemingly contradictory aspects of her past with the woman he saw before him now.

Lorelei didn't see his frown. She had turned away a moment before and was gesturing toward the interior of the house.

"Perhaps I should show you around first, so you can get an idea of what needs to be done."

"All right," Lucas said quietly as he followed her. She moved like a dancer, he thought, her carriage erect and with a subtle sway of her hips. Yet there was a certain delicacy about her, almost a fragility, that brought out his protective instincts, among other things. His body tightened, but he ignored it and instead took a careful look around.

There was no sign of the old lady who had answered the door the other day. As far as he could tell, Lorelei McGee was alone. That suited him fine. The fewer people who knew what he was doing, the better.

"The house dates from the late 1940s and early 1950s," Lorelei was saying. "It's modeled on a Venetian palazzo with two stories and a raised, colonnaded front. The red roof tiles were made in a small town near Venice. The marble used in the interior is blue-veined Carrara. There are about six thousand square feet in all, not big as these things go, but it was built with tremendous attention to detail. Every stone, every tile, every inch of plaster was perfect. Unfortunately, a lot has changed over the years."

"I can see that," Lucas said. He ran a hand over the wall near the entrance to the living room and grimaced. "It's damp. You've got a leak some-where."

"More than one. Pipes need to be fixed, and some of the wiring needs to be repaired." She led the way into the living room and pointed to the far end, where part of the floor had warped. "Some of the parquet has to be replaced and there's tons of paint-ing to be done. As I said in the ad, I can't pay much, but—"

She broke off, aware suddenly that Lucas wasn't listening to her. He had stopped right where he was and was staring at the opposite side of the room, near the large fireplace.

"Is that a . . . coffin?" he asked.

"What? Oh, that. Yes, I guess it is." Hastily she added, "But it was never actually used. I mean, ex-cept as a prop. It's from the movie *Hell House*. Did you ever see that one?"

Lucas nodded slowly, still eyeing the elaborate oak-and-brass box resting on a pedestal that was draped in burgundy velvet. The lid of the coffin was open, revealing an interior of puffed white satin that had yellowed slightly with age. Not exactly your everyday piece of living room furniture, but Lorelei seemed not to find anything odd about it at all.

"I saw it," he said, "when I was twelve. It scared the daylights out of me. I didn't sleep for two nights."

She smiled enthusiastically. "It was a great movie, wasn't it?" Without waiting for an answer, she went on, "My father kept a lot of mementos from his films. In a way, he turned this place into a museum. Eventually, I'll have to decide what to do with everything. But first I've got to get the house back in some kind of shape."

Lucas nodded. He presumed she realized that the most obvious problems needed to be fixed before she could get fair market value for the place. But what puzzled him was how they had developed to begin with and why she couldn't afford to spend much on repairs.

"I can do this work," he said when they had returned to the entry hall, "but it will take time. You could hurry things along by bringing in a crew."

"I can't afford that," she said, "but if you take the job, you won't be working alone. Believe me, I'll do my part."

Lucas hid his disbelief, but privately he thought, that would be the day. Princess McGee soil her hands trying to save a dilapidated mansion? When pigs could fly!

"I'll be back tomorrow," he said. "First thing should be to tackle the leaks, okay?"

"Fine," Lorelei said. "About your fee . . ."

He named a daily wage that was small enough to make her all but sag with relief. "That isn't much," she said. "Are you sure . . . ?"

He shrugged. "I like a challenge."

She wasn't about to argue with him. If he wanted to devote himself to fixing an old house, fine by her. She could only thank her lucky stars that he'd turned up when he had.

"Tomorrow then," she said. She watched for a moment as he walked away down the gravel drive, until she realized she was staring. Her cheeks were warm as she shut the door.

He was an unusual man, very self-contained and with an aura of unmistakable strength. She hardly knew him yet she found herself trusting him instinctively.

That scared her. If she had learned anything in life, it was to keep her emotions firmly in check. She'd been too bruised by personal experience to do anything else. Lucas Messina would come, he would paint and he would plaster, and do anything else that needed doing, but he would not penetrate the cocoon of self-sufficiency she had so carefully woven about herself. She wouldn't allow it.

Lorelei went back into the living room and from there to the den her father had used as an office. The dust was particularly thick there, as though Vincent McGee hadn't set foot in it for a considerable time before his death. Far off in the distance, a car motor sounded but Lorelei didn't notice.

She grimaced as she looked at the boxes stacked on the floor. She'd brought them up from the basement. They contained her father's financial records. Much as she hated the idea, she knew that she had to go through them. With a weary sigh, she sat down cross-legged on the floor, reached for the first box and began.

At the same time that Lorelei was contemplating boxes, Lucas was getting back into his car. He'd left it out of sight a discreet distance from the house. Before sliding behind the wheel, he took off his tool belt and tossed it in the back.

A wry smile touched his mouth. The belt wasn't much as disguises went, but it had done the job. Lorelei McGee believed he was what she wanted him to be—a skilled but not so terribly ambitious laborer looking for work. The impulse that had made him reply to her ad had paid off.

He'd seen it that morning as he was reading the paper over breakfast. In the days since Vincent's funeral, he'd come no closer to deciding how to deal with the dead man's daughter. His haughty dismissal from her doorstep had seemed to confirm everything he'd ever believed about the McGee family. But now he wasn't so sure.

The picture just didn't fit. There she was, alone in the house, worrying about finding the money to fix it up and glad to have his help. This wasn't the Princess McGee he knew about, the spoiled child of wealth and privilege who had flashed like a comet across the sky of the public's attention.

At seventeen, she'd been on the cover of *Vogue*, hailed as one of the world's most beautiful women. A few years later, all the supermarket tabloids had screamed the news of her affair with Hollywood's steamiest heartthrob. Not long after that, she'd disappeared from public view.

Now she was back, close at hand and unsuspecting of his true aims. He wanted the house as much as ever, but just then, driving along the shore road with the waves crashing on the rocky beach below, he admitted something else. He wanted Lorelei McGee, too.

At least long enough to solve the mystery of her.

Three

———

"I'm going to take some time off," Lucas said. He spoke matter-of-factly, as though this was an ordinary occurrence, but the two people listening to him didn't see it that way.

Sal was trying hard not to look worried. Lucas taking time off? Maybe to go into the hospital, but he couldn't think of any other reason.

"What's wrong?" he demanded, figuring what the heck, it was better to cut to the chase and risk getting his head handed to him than not to know how bad things were. Besides, Lucas was his cousin. He was family, and family had a right to be there when the you-know-what hit the fan.

"Nothing's wrong," Lucas said. He was sitting behind the worktable nearest the windows, with his chair pushed back and his long legs stretched out in front of him.

Lisa thought he looked relaxed and confident, but that didn't jive with the news he'd just imparted. Like Sal, she feared the worst.

"Whatever it is," she said sincerely, "you can count on us. We'll do anything you need."

Lucas shot her a wry look. "Am I really that bad? I tell you I'm going to take a little break and you both figure the roof is falling in?" He straightened in his chair and unconsciously drummed his fingers against the top of the table, a gesture that usually meant there was something he wasn't saying.

"It's a good time to get away," he insisted. "We've wrapped up a lot of work and everything that's still in hand is going great. Sal's planning a little trip, aren't you?"

The younger man nodded slowly. "I was, but now maybe I better reconsider. If you're—"

"Like hell," Lucas said. "You go telling Marie that you can't get away after all and I really will be in trouble. This is on the level, everything's fine. I just want a change of pace for a while."

"How long a while?" Lisa asked, ever practical. "Will I be able to reach you? What if there's an emergency?"

"Whoa," Lucas said. "I'm going to be right here in town. I can be here in five minutes if there's a problem."

The two of them exchanged a glance. "What kind of deal is this?" Sal demanded. "You're going to take the first vacation of your life and you're not even going away? Come on, Lucas, that isn't how it's done."

"So I'm new to this, sue me. The point is, you don't have to worry. Sal, go on your trip with Marie. Lisa, just keep doing what you always do. I'll be in touch every other day or so. There's nothing to worry about."

Neither one of them looked convinced, but at least they didn't argue any further. Five minutes later he was alone in his office, sorting through the last few items that couldn't wait until he got back.

He wasn't really sure when that would be, but he figured it couldn't be too long. He'd get into the house, get a good look around and make Lorelei a decent offer. Maybe she'd be mad when she realized he'd had an ulterior motive for taking her up on the job, but that was too bad. He'd never in his life gone into a deal blind and he wasn't going to start now, especially not when his emotions were involved.

Sal was right about that part—he was hung up on the McGee house. What his cousin didn't know— and what Lucas wasn't about to admit to anyone— was that Lorelei McGee had gotten under his skin. That was too bad, but it wouldn't be allowed to cloud his judgment.

His temper flared at the thought of what Vincent McGee had let happen to the house his father, uncles and grandfathers had sacrificed so much to build. Bad enough everything else that had happened, but at the absolute bottom, McGee should have taken decent care of the place. He hadn't, and that made Lucas see red.

Vincent wasn't around anymore, but Lorelei was. It fell to her to pay the piper. He was going to own the place and he was going to put it back the way it was supposed to be, but Vincent McGee's daughter wasn't going to get rich on the proceeds.

Half an hour later, having issued final assurances to Sal and Lisa that everything was all right, Lucas left the office. He was dressed in work clothes—jeans and an old shirt that he'd worn while painting his condo. He'd left the Cord in the garage and was driving a pickup that belonged to the business. A tool chest was in the back, along with a pile of tarps and a few old buckets.

He arrived shortly before 10:00 a.m., parked in front of the house and rang the bell. There was no answer. Surprised, since he presumed Lorelei was expecting him, he tried again. Still nothing. Frowning, he walked around the side of the house to the back door. It was unlocked.

Letting himself into the kitchen, he called out. "Miss McGee . . . ?"

A muffled sound reached him from somewhere deeper in the house. Letting the kitchen door close behind him, he followed the noise. To the right of the kitchen was a large pantry and beyond that was a built-in, restaurant-size freezer. Lucas remembered hearing about that freezer. It had been one of the first of its kind to be put into a private home. The door, large enough to get a small car through, was made of wood and crisscrossed by steel braces. Across the center was a bar that included, at one end, a steel handle. The door was securely closed. Muffled sounds and banging came from behind it.

Quickly, Lucas wrenched the door open. Lorelei fell into his arms. She was disheveled, wide-eyed and obviously glad to see him.

"Thank heavens," she gasped. "I kept telling myself that you'd be here, but I'm sure glad to know I was right."

"What the hell happened?" Lucas demanded. His arms tightened around her protectively as he stared over her head into the depths of the freezer. A wave of horror washed through him. How long had she been in there? How long would it have been before her air ran out?

"I was trying to find more of my father's records," she explained. "I knew he kept some stored in there, since it hasn't been used as a freezer in years. I went in there about a half hour ago, thinking there'd be no problem. There's supposed to be a safety latch to keep anyone from being trapped, but I guess it doesn't work any better than a lot of the other stuff around here." A shiver ran through her. "If you hadn't come..."

"Forget about it," he said gruffly. Without thinking, he cupped the back of her head and pressed her closer to him. He could feel her trembling as the terror she had held at bay while she was actually in danger came belatedly to the fore. The only colors in her face were her startlingly light blue eyes and the smattering of freckles across her nose. She looked very young and, for the moment at least, very much in need of comfort.

Lucas wouldn't have been a man if he hadn't responded. She felt so good against him, her slender body warm and lithe in his arms. He could smell the perfume of her hair, a mixture of honeysuckles, roses, sun and pure woman. Her high, firm breasts were pressed against his chest. For a moment, his arms tightened around her as a rush of passion seized him.

He inhaled sharply, struggling for control. She was Vincent McGee's daughter and she was a means to an end. Nothing more. He'd have to be crazy to forget that.

"I'm glad you're all right," he said as he deliberately set her away from him. His hands dropped from her shoulders. "I'll take that door off first thing. It's too dangerous to leave it on if the safety latch isn't working."

"All right," Lorelei replied. She met his gaze for an instant before looking hastily away. Warmth stained her cheeks. Her reaction amazed her. It was only natural that she was grateful to him, but what she was feeling went way beyond that. When he'd held her in his arms, when she'd felt the hard power of his body against hers, when . . .

She jerked her thoughts away from the tantalizing images that were forming in her mind. They were so unlike her that she hardly knew what to make of them.

"Thanks," she murmured as she turned to go. "I'll be upstairs... steaming wallpaper."

He nodded curtly but said nothing more as she beat a hasty retreat. When she was alone in the narrow hall that ran between the kitchen and the rest of the house, she paused to catch her breath.

Her heart was hammering and she could feel a strange tautness in her lower body. Much as she wanted to believe they were the result of her close brush with disaster, she couldn't manage it. Lucas Messina was turning out to be much more than she'd bargained for.

Heading for her bedroom, she was glad that the house was as large as it was and that she would be working at the far end of it, away from Lucas. The distance was mainly symbolic, but she needed time to herself to get control of her emotions.

The room had been hers as a child and was now hers as a young woman. It was large, with a high ceiling and windows that looked out toward the garden and the ocean. The furniture was the same she had always had—an 18th-century four-poster, wardrobe and dressing table—all brought from France, a rare Aubusson carpet in delicate shades of mauve and gray—and silk bed coverings hand-stitched in the famed workshops of Lyons.

Vincent McGee had believed in exposing his only child to refinement and elegance from an early age, so that she would be all the better able to appreciate them. Lorelei supposed it had worked, for she had an instinctive eye for quality. But she also had to admit that the result had been to set her apart from the vast majority of people her own age. She hadn't felt precisely lonely, but neither had she felt—nor did she feel—well connected to the world at large.

However, she could steam wallpaper with the best of them and that was exactly what she set herself to do. By the time noon rolled around, she had managed to block out everything else from her mind.

Her arms and shoulders ached from the weight of the steamer. Wet curlicues of discarded paper lay around her feet. The pattern had been a pretty one—primroses on a background of spring green—but the years had faded the print and made the paper so dry that it was gaping away from the wall in places. She had no choice except to remove it.

With one wall bared and another partly done, she set the steamer down with a sense of relief and rubbed her shoulders reflectively. She'd take a break and ask Lucas if he was ready for lunch. Politeness was ingrained in her; she couldn't do less than invite him to join her. Besides, she was convinced that their earlier encounter had been an aberration. Over tuna salad and lemonade, she expected to be her usual cordial but distant self.

She left the bedroom and was walking down the long, wide hallway that led to the stairs when a sudden crash froze her in place. Her first thought was that the freezer door had fallen, possibly on Lucas. Horrified, she dashed for the steps. When she reached the main floor, she could hear groaning coming from the kitchen. Heart pounding, she ran down the hall, only to come to a screeching halt at the scene that met her eyes.

Lucas was picking himself up from the floor, or at least trying to. A large painter's ladder lay next to him, where it had fallen. High above, near the ceiling, the door to one of the cabinets was swinging open.

Catching sight of her, Lucas grimaced. He got to his feet, glanced at the cabinet and shook his head disbelievingly.

"What's the matter?" Lorelei asked. She took a quick step toward him. "Are you hurt? What happened?"

"I lost my balance and fell," he said tautly, "but I'm fine. Everything's fine." Struggling for patience, he said, "I should have known better. The coffin was a dead giveaway."

Lorelei followed his gaze to the cabinet. When she saw what was inside, she groaned. "Oh, no, I forgot about that stuff."

"It's okay," Lucas said magnanimously. "I was up there checking the ceiling, the cabinet door swung open and I found myself looking at a collection of severed heads. But, hey, that kind of thing happens all the time. No sweat."

"They're from *Dr. Guillotine*. It was Dad's last movie."

"That explains it," Lucas said in a tone that suggested it didn't really. He eyed her cautiously. "Any more little surprises you care to tell me about?"

"I did mention that there were a lot of mementos," she reminded him gently. "They're pretty much scattered around the house. You shouldn't be surprised by anything you see." She didn't add that he also shouldn't be afraid because obviously you didn't say that to a man like Lucas Messina.

"I'll keep that in mind," he said gruffly as he righted the ladder. The motion stretched the fabric of his shirt across his broad, muscled back. Lorelei caught herself staring. She looked away hastily.

"I'm going to fix lunch. Join me?"

He hesitated a moment before he grinned. "Okay, provided we eat alone."

She laughed as they headed for the kitchen together, relieved that the incident was over.

"The terrace ought to be okay," she said as she opened the door leading onto it.

It was cool outside, but the terrace was sun-washed. The air had the special clarity of early spring caught at the moment of the world's awakening. They headed toward the old wrought-iron chairs beside the glass-and-iron table. The view looked out over the cliffs to the ocean beyond. A faint mist still lingered on the water, but closer in, near the rocks, a family of seals was at play.

"This could be a million miles from anywhere," Lucas said as he held out a chair for her.

"Sometimes I think it is," she said as she sat down. He came around the other side of the table to join her. The sun struck his raven hair, streaking it with silver. His shirtsleeves were rolled up to expose powerful forearms. He moved with easy grace and instinctive elegance that piqued her curiosity.

"How's it going so far?" she asked as she passed him the tuna salad.

"About how I expected. I've located half a dozen places where water's coming in. But I'm pretty sure the plumbing isn't the problem. It looks like there are chinks in the mortar of the outside walls. It wasn't repointed when it should have been. With a little luck, I'll find the trouble spots today and start fixing them tomorrow.''

"That fast?" Lorelei said, surprised. "I thought it would take longer."

Lucas shrugged. "The construction is solid. There are only a limited number of places where you can run into problems because of neglect. Around the window frames, for instance, or at the base of chimneys. I want to get up on the roof this afternoon and give it a good going-over." He smiled at her over the lemonade. "Any little mementos up there?"

She laughed and shook her head. It was strange sitting with him like this, feeling so comfortable. A tentative shyness clung to her, but she refused to give in to it. She had been alone for so long. The least she should be able to do was conduct a simple conversation with an attractive and pleasant man.

"I sure hope not," she said. "Want me to go up and check?"

He grinned wryly. "No thanks, I'll manage. After the heads, I think I'm ready for anything." He paused for a moment, looking at her thoughtfully. "It must have been a little strange, to say the least, growing up surrounded by things that are supposed to scare the daylights out of people. But you don't seem to be bothered by it at all."

"I guess it just goes to show that you can get used to anything," Lorelei admitted. "Besides, Dad always made sure that I knew none of it was real. The movies were just his way of whistling in the dark."

"So none of it scares you?"

"Not really."

"What does?"

Lorelei lowered her fork slowly. The question was unexpected and she wasn't sure how to reply. "What do you mean?"

"Everyone's afraid of something. If it's not prop coffins and latex heads, what is it?"

She stiffened. The sense of comfortableness was gone. She was suddenly wary. "Just the usual things, I suppose. Where did you learn so much about old houses?"

It was hardly a subtle way of changing the subject, but Lucas got the message. He filed away the information that Lorelei McGee was afraid of something she didn't care to discuss. That angered him on a visceral level, and the anger, in turn, baffled him. Why should he care?

"I've worked a lot of construction jobs," he said. "After a while, you get to see everything." He paused, looking at her, as he said, "Do you know anything about the people who built this house?"

"Not really. It was finished long before I was born. But I understand there was a family of craftsmen—Italian, I believe—that my father employed. They did a wonderful job."

"But you can't recall their name?"

A shadow passed behind her eyes. He spoke evenly, but she was catching whiffs of a strange, unexplained bitterness beneath his words that startled her. She must be wrong, but she could swear that he actually resented her forgetfulness.

"I'm not sure I ever heard it," she admitted. "As I said, it was all before my time."

He nodded, apparently satisfied with that. The rest of lunch passed amicably enough. But later, when she was back in the bedroom steaming off more of the wallpaper, she remembered his question about what frightened her.

A sad smile curved her mouth. Tony had always said the first rule of acting was to never let the bastards see you sweat. The same could be said of life in general. She had learned in the toughest school possible to keep her feelings strictly to herself, or—better yet—not to have any. The sole exception in recent years had been her love for her father, and he was gone.

But something else was stirring inside her, half-acknowledged as of yet, but clearly identifiable all the same. She desired Lucas Messina. He woke her to needs so long denied that she had followed herself into thinking she was immune to them. Now she was finding out that she was wrong.

The discovery frightened her, because it threatened all the safe moorings of her life. Without them, she would float out into a sea that seemed storm-tossed most of the time.

But here he was, in her house, in her life. Staring at the pretty wallpaper of her childhood as it came away in long, dying strips, she realized that she wasn't about to send him away.

Not yet, at least.

Four

Lorelei woke to the sound of the phone ringing. She groped for the receiver and put it to her ear, still half-asleep.

"Uh-umph?"

"It's Melly, dear," her aunt said. "Did I wake you?"

"Yes," Lorelei admitted. She knew she was supposed to deny she'd been asleep, people did that all the time, but she couldn't muster the energy.

In the four days since Lucas's arrival on the scene, she had spent almost every daylight hour working nonstop on the house. She was determined to do her part, just as she'd promised, but she also wanted to keep some distance between herself and the man who had come so unexpectedly into her life. There was a coiled strength about Lucas that made her feel at once protected and at risk. She preferred to stay so busy that she couldn't think about it.

The previous day she had finally finished steaming the last of the wallpaper from the upstairs bedrooms. The effort had left her aching in her bones. She turned over gingerly. "Where are you?"

"Acapulco. Thad and I decided to pop down for a visit in honor of your father. We all spent some happy times here."

"That's nice," Lorelei murmured.

"Of course, it's changed a great deal. So much more built-up than it used to be. But I said to Thad, darling Vincent would have enjoyed it all the more. He loved to see people having a good time and making money. Didn't he, dear?"

"I guess so," Lorelei said. She was fully awake now, although she wished she wasn't. A hot shower was what she needed, followed by about a gallon of coffee. But Melly wasn't done yet.

"How *are* you?" her aunt asked.

"I've been keeping busy working on the house."

"Very sensible of you, dear, as long as you don't overdo. By the way, I forgot to mention that you had a visitor the day before we left."

Lorelei frowned. She'd had lots of visitors. They'd come for the funeral, stayed as long as they thought necessary and left in a cloud of Arpege, champagne and tearful good cheer. "Who do you mean?" she asked.

"Marvelous-looking man, rather dark, very well built but just a shade sinister. Know him?"

Did she? Lorelei wasn't sure. The description could have fit Lucas, but why would he have come to the house before she'd even placed the ad? He had said he'd come in answer to her ad, hadn't he?

"I'm not sure," she said slowly. "Did he give a name?"

"No, he didn't. Darling, I'm afraid I was just a tad rude and it's been bothering me. But it was a stressful time, wasn't it? Besides, he did say he'd be back."

"I'll keep it in mind," Lorelei said. "Are you having a good vacation?"

"Marvelous," Melly assured her. Duty done, she was instantly cheerful. "Thad never changes. We danced the night away. He's rented a yacht and we've going sailing. Must run. I just wanted to make sure everything was all right."

Dancing, Lorelei thought after she had hung up. She got out of the bed and headed for the bath-room, shaking her head as she went. Sailing. Just who was who here? Thad and Melly were in their eighties, although neither would admit it. But they had more energy—and more fun—than just about anyone else she knew. Maybe she ought to take a leaf out of their book and try to relax a little.

Showered and dressed, she went downstairs, put on a pot of coffee and popped a muffin in the toaster. She had a long day of work ahead and needed the energy.

Lucas arrived a short time later. He found her sit-ting at the kitchen table, her hair caught back in a ponytail and a pensive look on her face.

"What's up?" he asked.

A little too quickly, she said, "Nothing. Want a cup of coffee?"

He nodded. "I'll get it." He'd found out the first day that she made coffee the way he liked it, strong enough to choke a horse. None of the namby-pamby stuff his employees were always trying to sneak through.

Taking a seat at the table, he said, "I'm going to get to work on the mortar this morning. When that's done, I'll take a look at the electrical system. You got lucky on the roof, by the way. I found a match for the tiles that are missing at a place not far from here and brought them along."

"That's great," she said, surprised that he'd been so successful. The tiles had been specially cast, after all. But she didn't doubt his word. All the work he'd done in the last few days had been meticulous. He seemed to care about the house as much as she did, which was truly remarkable.

Still looking at him, she asked, "By the way, did you happen to drop by here before my ad ran?"

Lucas didn't react visibly. He'd been prepared for the question, in fact had expected it. Unhesitantly, he said, "Yes, I did."

"Why?"

He shrugged. "I've always been curious about this house. It's really one of a kind."

"Then you saw my ad and came back?" she asked, struggling not to stare too obviously at the firm, chiseled shape of his lips. A small tremor ran through her as she suddenly wondered how they would feel pressed against her own.

"That's right." He looked at her steadily. "What's the matter?"

She smiled, a little embarrassed. "You'll have to forgive me. I was raised in a fishbowl. It's made me wary of people. But you have to admit, your turning up the way you did was very convenient."

"For both of us. You want work done and I want to do it, so what's the problem?"

"I guess there isn't any," she said slowly. "Is there?"

He took a sip of his coffee and felt a twinge of guilt. He wasn't being absolutely straight with her, having said nothing about his real interest in the house. But he was loath to tell her now. She was too vulnerable and too wary.

"Not as far as I'm concerned. Thanks for the coffee. I'm going to get started outside."

When he had left, Lorelei cleared away the remains of her breakfast. She was ready to start painting her bedroom, but thoughts of Lucas kept intruding.

If he was to be believed, he'd dropped by because he was curious about the house and, presumably, he'd left when he realized that her father had recently died. But how many people came to someone's front door because they happened to find it appealing? Of course, how many people were willing to work for the wages she could afford?

Was he simply different—a free spirit of a sort? Or did he have some ulterior motive?

She sighed, exasperated with herself as much as with the situation. Ever since Tony's death, she'd been so reluctant to take any chances. She'd pulled far back into herself, almost retreating from the world. It had worried her father, she knew that, although he had been immensely good about it. They'd stayed in close touch almost to the end.

And now—she was back, struggling to reclaim what was hers, and struggling, too, to come to terms with a man she was all too tempted to trust but wasn't sure that she should.

Meanwhile, Melly and Thad were in Acapulco having a blast.

She was definitely doing something wrong.

She went upstairs, discovered she had latex instead of oil-based paint, and cursed under her breath. It was turning out to be that kind of day.

Lucas was on a ladder near the front door, repairing the mortar around a window frame.

"I have to go into town," she said. "Do you need anything?"

"I'm fine."

"I'll be back in about an hour."

She got into her car, a sturdy four-wheel drive with no frills, and took off down the oceanfront road. The day was crisp and clear, warmer than it had been earlier in the week and so bright that just being out in it lifted her mood. She was smiling as she hung a left onto the main highway.

She didn't notice the car that got off at the same time and headed the way she'd come. But Lucas couldn't miss it a few minutes later when it crunched up the gravel driveway. He turned around on the ladder and looked at the man who got out from behind the wheel.

He was of medium height, sharply dressed, with watchful eyes and a salesman's smile.

"Hi, there," he said as Lucas came off the ladder. "I'm Jason Brandeis. Miss McGee around?"

"Not that I know of," Lucas hedged. He disliked the guy on principle. Anyone with shoes that shiny, for sure wanted more than the time of day.

"Maybe you have the wrong address," he added helpfully.

Brandeis looked him over, took in the work clothes and the mortar smeared on his hands, and let his smile go. Deadpan, he said, "Whatta you, work here?"

"You could say that. Lucas Messina." Deliberately, he stuck out a hand. Brandeis looked at it gingerly and backed off a few steps.

"Sorry, buddy, no offense, but I got to watch out for the wardrobe. Listen, you could do me a favor. I've really got to run this McGee broad to ground and this is the only address I got on her. Her old man croaked last week so I figure she ought to be here. Am I right or am I right?''

''Depends,'' Lucas said. He let his hand drop as his mind sorted through the possibilities, none of them good—IRS, subpoena server, private eye. Or maybe somebody doing collections for a friendly neighborhood loan shark.

Brandeis looked stumped for a moment before he started to nod. ''I get you. Hey, why not? Spread it around.'' He reached into his jacket pocket for his wallet and pulled out what looked to be a twenty. ''So what's the story?''

Lucas looked at the money, looked again at Brandeis and laughed. ''That rules out loan shark. Probably IRS, too, although you never can tell with them.''

Mr. Wardrobe looked genuinely horrified. ''Hey, no way. I'm strictly legit. I work for the *Inquisitor.* You know it?''

Lucas nodded slowly. He'd seen the so-called newspaper plenty of times at the checkout counter of the supermarket. Come to think of it, he'd never known anyone who admitted to buying it, but somebody sure was, since its circulation topped even the more successful weeklies, those that couldn't find room for the latest on alien landings, Elvis sightings

and the doings of various stars, starlets, boy toys and
wannabes.

The IRS would have been better—if only by a hair.

"Miss McGee isn't here," he said.

Brandeis put the twenty away, but he looked
skeptical. "You know her?"

"Some."

"So where is she?"

"Not here."

"Hey, come on. What's with the cold shoulder?
This is Princess McGee we're talking about. She was
running with the Hollywood brat pack before she
was fifteen, hit the cover of *Vogue*—gimme a
break—two years later and shacked up with Tony
Mancuso not long after that. This is not some
shrinking violet. The protective routine is real
touching, but it's out of place."

Lucas smiled. He looked completely relaxed, as
though he was enjoying himself. Only someone who
knew him real well—Sal, for instance—would have
seen what was in his eyes. And run like hell.

"Oh, yeah? You think so?"

Brandeis nodded vigorously. "Believe me, she
knows her way around the block. So what's the deal?
She holed up here or not?"

"I told you," Lucas said nicely, "she isn't here.
And now I'm going to tell you something else."

He walked over to Brandeis, took hold of him and lifted him off the ground. Worse yet, he did it effortlessly. All those summers hauling concrete on construction projects, all those long days and nights lifting lumber, hammering nails, shoveling fill, had put him in the kind of condition no gym jock or steroid freak could hope to equal.

With his feet dangling in the air, Brandeis grimaced. Nobody worked for the *Inquisitor* without getting used to a certain amount of abuse, but this was beyond the call of duty. The guy holding him looked like he was maybe an inch away from a major felony.

"Whoa! Let's not turn this into something it shouldn't be. You don't want me around, that's fine. I'm outta here. I'm history."

Lucas's smile deepened. He nodded approvingly. "That's good. You're not as dumb as you look. But before you go, just one thing. You do understand what will happen if you ever come back here?"

Brandeis moved his head up and down to signify that, oh, yes, he had indeed gotten the message, had in fact incorporated it into his very soul, and he could not imagine ever returning under any circumstances. Honest.

"So," he said after Lucas had lowered him back to the ground, "she couldn't just get an attack dog?"

He ran a finger around his shirt collar. "A nice rott-weiler, maybe, one that had chewed up a few people and needed a new home? That wasn't good enough for her? She had to get you instead?"

Lucas sighed, as though summoning what would surely be the absolute last of his patience. "Do we need to talk some more?"

"No," Brandeis said hastily. He started backing away toward his car. "Nope, not us, not ever again. But, hey, just in case you change your mind, the re-lationship goes sour, or you don't get enough kib-ble, whatever, here's my card."

He held it out, realized Lucas wasn't going to take it and laid it on the grass. "Night or day, the *Inquisitor* never sleeps. We also pay good. Forget the twenty, I'm talking real money. So—"

"We do need to talk some more," Lucas said, taking a step forward.

Brandeis held up his hands. "Gotta run. There's a woman in Portland says she bought a head of cab-bage with Elvis's face on it." He shrugged. "Who knows, could happen."

He jumped in the car, hit the ignition and took off. Lucas waited until the dust settled, then shook his head ruefully. He was heading back toward the lad-der when he remembered Brandeis's card.

Since his mother had always told him not to litter, he picked it up and put it in his shirt pocket. He'd get rid of it later. First, he had to decide what he was going to tell Lorelei when she got home.

Five

Lucas waited until much later in the day, when it was getting on for him to leave, before he said anything about Lorelei's visitor. She was out behind the house, cleaning brushes as he came up to her.

They'd seen little of each other since her return; he'd been busy outside and down in the basement checking over the wiring, while she'd been painting the bedroom. There was a smudge of paint on her cheek and a few drops in her hair as she looked up at him now.

''Ready to go?'' she asked.

"Just about. Listen, while you were out, a guy dropped by, name of Brandeis. Said he's from the *Inquisitor*. He wanted to talk to you."

Lorelei set down the brush she'd been cleaning and stood up slowly, wiping her hands on her jeans.

"How come you didn't say anything before?"

"Slipped my mind," he lied. The truth was he knew she wasn't going to like it and he'd put it off as long as he could because of that. Now, looking at her, he knew he'd been right. If anything, he'd underestimated her reaction. She'd gone pale and her hands trembled.

"I should have expected this," she said, almost to herself.

"How come?"

"Because it's happened before."

"You mean you know him?"

She shook her head wearily. "No, not him personally. But I know how he works, the same way they all do. Anyone they can latch onto, make a story out of, isn't even a person to them. They'll exploit anything, twist anything, invent anything just to get what they want."

She sounded as though she was speaking from experience, Lucas thought grimly. He was starting to regret that he hadn't been tougher on Brandeis.

Meaning to reassure her, he said, "He won't be back."

Lorelei looked doubtful. "Sure he will. What's to stop him?"

Lucas shrugged. "I told him not to come back."

Her eyes widened slightly. "What makes you think he'll listen?"

"He was hanging about two feet off the ground at the time."

Now her eyes were really big, crystalline blue saucers that seemed to take up most of her face. A tiny smile started to quiver around the corners of her mouth.

"You're kidding?"

He ducked his head slightly, hoping she wasn't going to make a big deal out of it. He wasn't used to playing Sir Galahad. "I just made a suggestion, that's all."

"While holding him in midair?"

"What can I tell you? He rubbed me the wrong way." He didn't add that what had particularly irked him was the reference to her shacking up with Tony Mancuso. It was no secret, but for some reason he didn't like having his nose shoved in it.

Lorelei shot him a long, level look. Slowly the tension in her began to ease. "Well, how about that," she said softly.

"I'm normally a very nice guy," he said defensively.

She kept right on looking at him. "Uh-huh." She thought things over for a moment before she said suddenly, "We skipped lunch and I'm starved. Would you like something to eat?"

It was his turn to smile. He was surprised, but also pleased. Four days he'd known this woman and already it was hard to walk away from her. "I have to get cleaned up first."

"Go ahead. I'll meet you in the kitchen."

He could feel her still watching him as he walked back around the side of the house.

Twenty minutes later, when Lucas came into the kitchen, Lorelei was standing at the counter slicing vegetables for a salad. He had washed and changed into a clean shirt that he'd had in the truck. She had also taken the time to put on a fresh blouse and slacks. The paint was gone from her cheek and her hair was brushed so that the deep golden tints within it gleamed like captured rays of sun.

Lucas shook his head at the thought. He was getting downright poetic, which worried him. Around Miss Lorelei McGee, he'd be smart to keep his head clear.

"Can I help?" he asked.

"No, thanks. There's beer in the fridge. Why don't you just relax? It's been a long day."

Lucas didn't have to be asked twice. Much as he hated to admit it, he had spent too much time lately repointing mortar. It was tough, tedious work and he was glad it was over.

"I did get to the basement," he said as he sat down. "The fuse box looks okay. The wiring's adequate, but if you wanted to put in air-conditioning or anything like that, it would have to be updated."

"I'll remember that," Lorelei said. She tossed the salad in a bowl and checked the large pot of water on the stove. While she waited for it to boil, she slipped a loaf of Italian bread into the oven.

"So," she said as she got a package of pasta from the refrigerator, "you didn't have any problem in the basement?"

"Should I have?" Lucas asked.

"It was one of Dad's favorite spots for squirreling things away."

He grimaced. "That explains it. I did notice lots of old boxes and trunks, stuff kind of covered over with blankets, but I headed straight for the fuse box and straight out again. There could be anything down there and I wouldn't know it."

"Anything and everything," Lorelei agreed. "I still haven't figured out what I'm going to do with all of it."

"How about a tag sale?" Lucas asked, half kidding.

"Actually, that's not a bad idea. Heaven knows, I could use the money and there are probably plenty of people who would appreciate a bit of memorabilia from the Master of Horror."

"How come the Master didn't leave you in better shape?" Lucas asked.

"Dad wasn't much good with money," she said simply. "It came, it went. Anyway, I'll get around to clearing things out eventually."

He was glad to hear that, since he had no desire to take over the house complete with coffin, heads and who-knew-what-else. But it didn't seem like a good time to mention that.

Instead he asked, "Does it bother you, staying here by yourself?"

Lorelei looked surprised. "Why should it? This was my home for most of my life."

It was also a big, lonely house full of weird stuff, but she didn't seem to see it that way. "It's kind of isolated," Lucas pointed out, "don't you think?"

"I'm used to that. Don't get me wrong, I miss Dad. But he would have been the first one to tell you that he'd had a good long run. It's different when—'' She caught herself and broke off.

Quickly she dumped the pasta into the water and gave it a stir.

"When is it different?" Lucas asked, watching her.

She flicked the fire off under the pasta, slipped oven mitts on her hands and took the pot over to the sink where she dumped it out into a strainer.

"When it's a young person who dies," she said, her back to him. She spoke without emotion, simply stating a fact. "Would you give the sauce a stir?"

He obliged as she carried the pasta to the table. A few minutes later they were ready to eat. At Lorelei's suggestion, Lucas had opened a bottle of wine. He poured a glass for her as he said, "It's nice of you to do this. I'm not much of a cook myself and there are times when I think I can't stand any more fast food."

"That stuff can kill you," she said seriously. "Besides, if you don't mind my turning the tables a little, how come there's no wife at home making sure you watch your cholesterol?"

Lucas broke off a piece of warm bread and laid it on his plate. "That your way of telling me I ask too many personal questions and now it's your turn?"

"You do get one in every once in a while. But all I know about you is that you've been around here long enough to be aware of this house and that you seem to know a lot about construction. Oh, yes, and there's a guy named Brandeis who probably isn't too fond of you. But there must be more."

"I grew up around here," Lucas said. He chose his words with care. "I left when I was eighteen and about two years ago I came back. There is a Mrs. Messina. As a matter of fact, there's a bunch of them, starting with my mother and including my three sisters-in-law. I know a lot about construction because that's all I've ever done. Satisfied?"

Not by a long shot, Lorelei thought, but she wasn't about to say so. For one thing, she was too busy mulling over the little shock of dismay that had ripped through her when he'd said there was a Mrs. Messina, not to mention the flood of relief that had followed when he explained what he meant by that.

She had the sinking feeling that she was getting in over her head, but for the life of her, she couldn't figure out what to do about it. After being self-sufficient for so long, it was bewildering to feel so drawn to another person. Lucas Messina appealed to her in too many ways. He made her feel at once safer than she ever had and yet tremulously excited, which made no sense at all.

She twirled the pasta on her fork, but made no attempt to eat it. Instead she said, "It sounds like you come from a large family."

"More of a clan, actually. Were you an only child?"

She nodded. "My parents married late in my father's life. I gather I was a surprise."

"Your mother was some kind of heiress from Boston, wasn't she?"

Lorelei laughed and shook her head. She wasn't surprised that he knew. It had been common knowledge at one time, along with much more about Princess McGee.

"So she liked to claim, but the closest she ever got to Boston was when she ate baked beans. Her name was Maybelle Lestand. She came from somewhere down in Texas, and she hotfooted it out of here not too long after I was born."

"I'm sorry," Lucas murmured. "But you don't seem to mind much."

"I've had plenty of time to get used to it. Besides, everybody has something in their life they wish could have been different."

"Probably," Lucas agreed. "Is that it in your case? If there was one thing you could change, it would be your mother?"

Lorelei shook her head slowly. "I never knew her, so she just isn't that important. No, what I'd change—"

"What you said before, about someone dying young?"

Sadness flickered behind her eyes. "There's no point talking about it."

Lucas took a bite of pasta. It was good, but he hardly tasted it. Nor did he want any more. His stomach felt knotted.

He looked at her for a long moment, watching the play of light and shadow over her face. His life was on course; he was getting everything he'd worked for. She was a complication he just didn't need.

And simply couldn't resist. Abruptly, Lucas made up his mind. He put his fork down, stood up and walked around to her side of the table. Her eyes were wide as she watched him. He bent and gently cupped her face in his hands. She offered no resistance but continued to stare at him cautiously.

"I have to know," he murmured, his breath warm on her skin. "What you make me feel, is it an illusion or is it real?"

Lorelei had no answer for him, not just then. She was too caught up in the suddenness of it all, the surprise and above all the surging gladness. He wasn't the only one who had been wondering and waiting.

His mouth brushed hers. His touch was warm, firm, not yet demanding but with a hint of far more to come. Instinctively she responded, flowing upward into his arms. They clung together as the kiss deepened. The taste of him filled her—crisp, slightly fruity from the wine, utterly masculine. She made a low sound in her throat and clung to him even tighter. The languorous, stroking touch of his tongue sent undulating waves of pleasure through her. Her eyes fluttered shut as sweet, hot desire claimed her.

Long moments passed before Lucas shakily raised his head. His eyes were storm-darkened, lit with surprise as he surveyed her flushed face and slightly bruised mouth. He took a deep breath, struggling for control, and said the first thing that came into his mind.

"You aren't still in love with Tony Mancuso, are you?"

Six

"You really missed out, Messina," Lorelei said. "You should have been a diplomat." She jerked away from him, more hurt and confused than she could admit, and sat down. It was either that or risk her legs not holding her.

Lucas sighed and took his own seat again. He reached for the bottle of wine to refill her glass. "Okay, so I'm not subtle, but everybody knew you were involved with the guy, plus you were real young, so it must have hurt like hell when what happened to him happened. You said yourself, it's worse when a young person dies."

"He didn't die," Lorelei said. She took a sip of the wine, decided it was better than she thought and took another. "Don't you know that Tony Mancuso still lives in the hearts of all his many fans?"

"That sounds like something Brandeis would write, but even if it's true, what's the harm?"

"The harm is what it did to him. Tony was a nice guy in a business where people like that usually wind up as lunch. He made it to the top for the simple reason that he was really good and he really cared."

"So he was a saint. How old were you when you met him?"

"Sixteen."

Lucas made a sound deep in his throat. "How old was he?"

"Twenty-eight."

"Oh, great, a twenty-eight-year-old man and a sixteen-year-old girl. Some saint. You realize you were just over the wire on statutory rape."

Lorelei laughed shakily. "You don't get it."

"Yeah, I think I do."

Her eyes met his across the table. He was angry and he didn't want to show it, but the idea of her with Tony Mancuso, especially as young as she'd been, drove him nuts. What the hell had Mr. Movie Star been thinking of to take up with anybody that vulnerable?

"Tony was my friend," she said softly.

"I'll bet."

"He was the best thing that ever happened to me."

Lucas's eyes narrowed. Okay, the guy was dead and maybe entitled to be cut a little slack because of it. But could she really still be so naive?

"He was a grown man taking advantage of a kid. Where was your father while all this was going on? What was he thinking of?"

"Dad had a stroke when I was fifteen. It took him a long time to recover. While he was doing it, I fell in with the wrong crowd. Tony fished me out."

"Tony the hero. He made it big in the movies, got lost little girls to trust him and ended up going off the side of a cliff. One of nature's noblemen."

Lorelei stiffened. "Did it ever occur to you—just once—that you might be wrong about something? You never knew Tony and you sure don't know me." Her voice shook. "But you're like all the others, jumping to the worst possible conclusions."

His fists clenched on the table. It was eating him up inside, that she still cared so much for a man long dead. What did you say to a woman who felt that way? How did you make her realize there was more to life than—

What in God's name was he thinking about? He was there for the house, nothing else. If she wanted to carry a torch, what difference did it make to him?

Angry—because it all too plainly did make a difference—he said, "Wise up, McGee. He took advantage of you when you were young and innocent, and you put him in a shrine for doing it. I give him credit, he had good taste, but you ought to know better."

She paled, which made him feel rotten, but he couldn't bring himself to back down. He felt like a stranger to himself, as though he couldn't predict or control what he would do next. For a man who had always managed to rise above emotion, the effect was almost terrifying.

Lorelei put her fork down carefully, adjusted her wineglass just so and glared at him. "I give *you* credit, Messina. You've got all the sensitivity of that mortar you were slapping around today *and* you've got the brains to match. Now if you'll excuse me, I've lost my appetite."

The slight stung. She was suddenly not the woman who cooked pasta for him and laughed about what was in her basement, but the Ice Princess, looking down on the help when they had the gall to step out of line. Maybe it wasn't the most mature response of his life, but there it was and he had to deal with it.

"Suits me," he shot back as he crumbled his napkin, tossed it on the table and rose. "Good night."

The door slammed behind him.

Lorelei sat at the table, staring blankly at the discarded dishes. Several minutes passed before she managed to rouse herself. The sudden silence rang in her ears. She took a deep, shaky breath and pressed her lips together hard. Her eyes burned.

She was acting like an idiot, that was all there was to it. The strain of her father's death, the need to confront her own past in the house and the worry over how she was going to save the place had all combined to undermine her defenses. Otherwise Lucas Messina would never have been able to get to her the way he did.

She'd been too hard on him. He couldn't be blamed for believing the gossip about her and Tony. Everybody else believed it, too. That she wanted more from Lucas wasn't his fault. It didn't even make any sense.

She cleared the dinner away, wiped the counters and swept the floor before she finally ran out of things to do. The solitude weighed down on her as she made her way to the living room. It looked big, empty and uninviting. With the paint still wet in her former bedroom, there was no place in all the house where she could go for comfort.

Her throat was tight as she pulled on a jacket and wandered outdoors. It was dark, but a full moon illuminated the lawns—or what would be lawns someday when she got around to resurrecting them. Off in the distance she could make out the looming shapes of the yews that screened the house from the road.

Following a narrow gravel path, she walked around the house to the side facing the ocean. Behind what had been formal gardens was a small gazebo, glowing white beneath the silvered moon. Lorelei had spent many happy afternoons there reading and daydreaming.

She settled herself on a bench looking out toward the water. The night was warm and the air was fragrant with the scents of grass and trees. She closed her eyes and leaned her head back, instinctively seeking the peace she had always found in this place.

But this time it wouldn't come. She could think only of Lucas. He pierced her solitude in a way she would never have imagined possible. He made her feel vulnerable in a way she had never before experienced. Everything she thought she knew was turned upside down by the mere thought of him.

She smiled wanly to herself. If this was what it was like to be attracted to another person, no wonder it caused so much trouble. It was a wonder anyone got anything done while going around in such a state.

Not her, though. She was going to put it all aside, go back to being her normal self-contained self and get on with life. Any minute now she was going to get up, march back into the house and read the instructions of the floor sander. Any minute.

Lucas put the key in the truck's ignition, started to turn it and stopped. He sat, staring out through the windshield. This was crazy. It was completely unlike him to be so uncertain. It was even rarer for him to be tied up in knots over a woman. Worse yet, a woman who was carrying a torch for a dead guy.

But there he was, unable to drive away and leave Lorelei.

With a muttered curse, he got out of the pickup and headed toward the house. The front door was locked—at least she had had enough sense to do that—but the side one was open. The kitchen was empty.

"Lorelei?" he called.

His voice seemed to go on forever in the huge, silent house. There was no answer.

The dinner dishes were in the sink, the table had been completely cleared. He couldn't hear water running anywhere, nor was there any other indication that she was in the house.

Frowning, he went back outside and stared into the darkness. Off in the distance behind the house, he caught a glimpse of white. He moved toward it and realized that he was looking at a small building, a gazebo. There was someone inside.

Lorelei was sitting with her back to him. Her shoulders were slumped and even without being able to see her face, he could sense the unhappiness in her. His stomach tightened.

"Lorelei," he said again, more softly.

She stiffened and turned her head, meeting his eyes. Her own were large with surprise.

"You came back."

He nodded curtly as he crossed the small distance between them and climbed the steps to the gazebo. She was all in shadows, only her face standing out against the night, like a sculpture encountered in some hidden place. There was a stillness in her, like the deep flowing of an ancient river, but he sensed that there was turbulence, as well, as if her emotions washed over sharp rocks that could not be avoided.

"I didn't want to leave you upset," he said.

Her eyes dropped, hiding her thoughts. He hesitated before taking a seat next to her. Below, he could hear the ocean crashing against the shore. A breeze fluttered past, laden with the scents of far-off places.

"I owe you an apology," she said quietly.

Lucas was surprised. He'd figured it for the other way around. "How come?"

She shifted slightly on the bench. "I wasn't honest with you about Tony. You're not to be blamed for thinking the same as everyone else."

His frown deepened. "I should have listened better. Was he really just your friend?"

Lorelei nodded. "I wasn't kidding when I said he pulled me out of a bad situation. He was like the older brother I never had. That was all we wanted, to be friends. But the gossip columnists, the tabloids, everyone insisted on making it into something it wasn't. It's an old story. I saw my father and his friends go through it, so I didn't have any trouble understanding what was happening with Tony. They sold their souls for the success, the fame, the accolades. They ended up not even belonging to themselves anymore, and then, when they found out they didn't like the results, there was nothing they could do about it except try to find a way out."

"Is that what your father did," Lucas asked slowly, "coming up here and building this house?"

Lorelei nodded. "He knew his ideas about movies were going out of fashion. Instead of good, wholesome horror, where it was all make-believe and no one ever really got hurt, it was all turning very savage, very real. It hurt him to be told he basically wasn't wanted anymore, but at least he had a good run while it lasted. Tony was just at the beginning of his run, when he realized he couldn't handle it anymore.''

"Why? Look, I don't know much about the guy, but he was some kind of romantic heartthrob, wasn't he? Women were hanging all over him. What exactly was so tough about that?"

Lorelei laughed under her breath. "You don't think that's tough, all those women hanging around?"

Lucas cleared his throat. He'd walked right into that one. "Well, no," he admitted. "I mean, there are worse things. A young guy, single, probably wouldn't think that was so bad."

"There was just one catch. Tony was gay."

Lucas eyed her narrowly. She had to be kidding. "Tony Mancuso? Mr. Every American Woman's Dream? He was gay?"

"Sure was." She was amazed to find herself speaking so openly after having kept the secret for so long. But something about this man inspired trust.

"He didn't set out to try to fool anyone," she went on softly. "It wasn't his fault the way things happened. His first big break came in a soap opera, where he wasn't even supposed to be a main character. But somehow he caught on, the viewers started writing in, and his part got beefed up. All of a sudden he found himself cast as a leading love interest. Tony was a really good actor, and he had a great ability to understand other people's feelings. He played the role to the hilt, and his career took off like a rocket. The only problem was that if he wanted to hold on to it, he had to play the same role offscreen as well as on. Otherwise, he'd lose everything."

"So you helped him," Lucas murmured. It was starting to make sense now, the inexplicable mixture of sophistication and innocence that he felt in her, why she didn't come across as the spoiled Princess McGee he'd expected.

"I realized how vulnerable he was, how easily someone could take advantage of his situation, and I wanted to pay him back at least a little for the help he'd given me."

"He was lucky to have you for a friend," Lucas said. He was feeling a whole lot more charitable toward Tony Mancuso now. Wherever the guy was, he wished him well. But something still didn't quite fit.

"After he died, you dropped out of sight. With him gone, you just couldn't handle being in that world?"

She shook her head. "I didn't want to be in it anymore. Besides, I—" She broke off and looked away from him.

"You what?" Lucas asked. He wasn't sure when he'd come to sit so close to her, so close that he could feel the slender line of her thigh along his own. The warmth of her body enclosed him. He shut his eyes for a moment, fighting for control.

"Nothing," Lorelei said. She turned her head slightly. Her hair brushed his arm. "Lucas—"

It was all happening so blindingly fast for them both. Lucas struggled to hold on to reason, but Lorelei had always been in the back of his mind, ever since he'd seen that cover of *Vogue* so many years before—Vincent McGee's beautiful Ice Princess daughter. Nothing had changed and yet everything had. Sweet heaven, he wanted her.

His hand moved along the lithe curve of her waist, up her back to cup her head. Warm, silken curls smelling of flowers and moonlight tangled around his questing fingers. Her eyes were wide and luminous, reflecting the rising moon. He hesitated for the space of a heartbeat before need, so unexpected and so overwhelming, engulfed them both.

His head lowered, his lips teasing hers. She made a soft sound deep in her throat. He moved slightly on the bench, lifting her easily until she was cradled on his lap. Her arms twined around his neck as her breasts pressed against his chest. A tremor ran through him as his body tightened convulsively.

The kiss grew more demanding. His lips parted hers, his tongue seeking the sweet, moist warmth of her. Her teeth raked him lightly. He groaned and let his hands wander over the high, full curve of her breasts. She wore a thin silk blouse that denied him little.

She drew back slightly, gazing into his eyes for an instant before she returned his kiss with unbridled passion. Beneath her buttocks she could feel his arousal rising hard and demanding. A jolt of shock went through her, but she ignored it, preferring instead the heady, mindless passion that was carrying her along toward a destination she could not glimpse but instinctively sensed.

His fingers fumbled on the buttons of the blouse. It parted beneath his touch. He slipped the cool silk from her honeyed shoulders and let it pool around her waist. Beneath, she wore only a lacy bra. She gasped faintly as he opened it, spreading the lace to either side so that he could gently, almost reverently, cup her breasts in his callused palms.

Her head fell back as waves of pleasure washed through her. His thumbs raked over her nipples, bringing them to aching fullness. Had it not been for the strength of his arms holding her, she would have fallen. Effortlessly he moved her closer, making her startlingly aware of the fullness of his arousal pressing against her bottom. His head lowered, dark against the night. She cried out softly as his mouth took first one and then another nipple, suckling hard even as his hands stroked the bare length of her back.

This was madness, Lorelei thought. She had never in her life done anything so impulsive or so wanton. Yet she seemed unable to stop herself. Bereft of reason, unable to draw away from the man who touched her so profoundly, she gave up the struggle. This night, at this moment, she put aside the strictures of a lifetime and cast herself adrift in a sea of sweeping dreams and surging hopes.

Her nipples were full and aching when he lifted his head again. She could see the heat in his cheeks, in his eyes, in the tightening of his mouth as he gave her a final chance to retreat. With a calmness she was far from feeling, she met his gaze and smiled.

Seven

———

Lucas stood with her in his arms, but he didn't carry her into the house. There were still too many memories there and too many complications. Instead he stepped outside the gazebo and laid her down on the thick, fragrant grass.

He told himself to go slowly, but the beauty of this woman and the wonder of the moment threatened to overwhelm him. He came down beside her, cupping her face in his hands, and dropped light, urgent kisses over her forehead, near the delicate corners of her eyes and along her damask smooth cheeks. The soft sounds of pleasure she made drove him further.

Unable to bear even the slight barrier that remained between them, he took her hand and slipped it under his shirt. The touch of her fingers against his heated skin made his body tighten almost painfully. His head arched, the muscles of his neck cording. His breathing was ragged as he took her other hand and brought it to join the first.

Despite her inexperience, Lorelei needed no further urging. Being with him like this banished all restraint and hesitation. Her fingertips tingled as she stroked the hard, heated skin lightly overlaid with softly curling hair. He felt like velvet over granite, so different from herself. Yet here, in his arms, she was discovering a part of her own nature too long lost to her.

In the dark scented night they found each other. Swiftly, they stripped away their garments, hands fumbling with buttons and zippers. Quickly, quickly, delay was unbearable. Every instant seemed altered beyond the ordinary, drawn out, lit with startling clarity, everything so obvious, so simple, so utterly necessary.

Naked, they lay together on the moist grass, touching, caressing, tasting, until so swiftly the fire caught and Lorelei cried out, gathering him to her in a gesture both ancient and instinctive. Tension drew his features taut as he rose above her, holding himself in strict check, waiting . . . until at last he could wait no more and his control, so long nurtured and so much a part of him, abruptly shattered.

He moaned her name as he thrust deep within her, heedless now of everything but the single, driving force that compelled him to unite with this woman in the most fundamental way possible. Her eyes widened as the brief shock of possession gave way to surging pleasure. Then her hips lifted, drawing him deeper. Moonlight washed over them both, silvering the straining tips of her breasts, the long, powerful arch of his back, the graceful, strong bodies moving in perfect oneness.

And moonlight, dipping over the yews and along the foam-crested waves, shone on them gently when at last passion crested and they slumped, exhausted, in each other's arms.

A long time later, Lorelei stirred. Lucas was a welcome heaviness against her. His eyes were closed, the lashes lying darkly against his cheeks. She smiled as she saw the soft parting of his lips, the faint flush of his skin, the tumbled disarray of his hair, and glimpsed, for just a moment, the child he had been.

Odd, she thought, shaking her head, to think of such a thing just then. Or perhaps it was the nature of the business—the man so proudly virile, dominant within her only to expend himself and be, for however short a time, weakened by the draining of his life.

Whereas she felt—how exactly? Astounded? Joyful? Relieved? All that and more. She felt freed in the most remarkable way from her own doubts and insecurities, as though the shadows of a lifetime had finally been banished. She was no longer simply Vincent McGee's daughter, sheltered and pampered, but kept also from the real world. Nor was she Tony's friend, struggling uselessly to help him against challenges she only dimly understood and was not remotely capable of dealing with.

Instead she was finally and irrevocably the woman she had tried to become in the four years away from home, strong, independent, secure, ready for a man like Lucas Messina. Presuming, of course, that he was "like" anything. Given the most recent evidence, she was willing to believe he was unique.

Lucas raised his head, saw the look in her eyes and smiled with pardonable complacency. Huskily he said, "Next time you decide to turn the world upside down, could you give me a little warning?"

She laughed, suddenly shy again, and reached for her clothes. He lay on the grass, his head propped on a hand, and watched unabashedly as she slid the silk blouse back on, along with her panties. It seemed pointless to bother with anything else.

A lock of ebony hair fell over his forehead, giving him a rakish look. As he brushed it aside, she said, "At the risk of sounding mundane, the temperature's falling. If you lie there much longer, you risk freezing your you-know-what off." She smiled. "And it's such a cute you-know-what."

Lucas laughed. He vaulted to his feet, reached for his jeans and pulled them on. Hand in hand, they walked back to the house.

"Does the fireplace in the living room work?" Lucas asked when they were once again inside.

Lorelei nodded. "I tried it the other night and it works fine."

"Good. Do you mind if I get a fire started?"

She resisted the urge to tell him that he already had. "Sounds good. How about I see what can be done with dinner?"

Lucas's stomach answered for him with an audible growl. He had the grace to look abashed.

"Go on," she said softly. "We can eat in front of the fire."

By the time she had cooked fresh pasta, reheated the sauce and warmed the bread again, the pungent scent of wood smoke floated on the air. Piling everything, including a bottle of wine, onto a tray, she carried it down the hall to the living room.

Lucas was on his knees, putting another log on the fire. Golden light suffused his bare chest and back. She stopped for a moment and simply stared at him. He filled the big, dusty room with life. And for the first time in a very long while, she let herself realize how alone she had been.

He turned at the sound of her step and smiled when he saw what she was carrying.

"Who else is coming?" he teased as he stood to help her.

"You sounded hungry."

"I am," he admitted. Together they unloaded the dishes onto a low table in front of the fire. Lucas popped the cork on the wine and filled their glasses. Sitting cross-legged, they drank a toast.

"Here's looking at you, kid," he said.

They ate in companionable silence, both suddenly ravenous. When the food was gone, they stretched out in front of the fire with their backs to one of the couches. Lucas's chest was warm and bare beneath her cheek as Lorelei snuggled against him. She felt safer and more content than ever before in her life.

When his dark head lowered, she welcomed his kiss, savoring the spicy wine taste of him, the strength of his arms, the extraordinary, soaring sense that she had somehow, after all these years, truly come home.

Their mouths met again and again. Playfully, teasingly, they enjoyed each other. His big hands stroked the length of her, cupping her buttocks gently, pressing her close so that she felt his arousal and shivered with pleasure. When he drew her to him, the touch of his hair-roughened chest against her nipples made her gasp softly. Muscles clenched deep within her as she strained toward him, all reticence gone.

When he lifted and carried her up the stairs to her room, she offered no protest. In the big four-poster, they found each other again, banishing doubt, eliminating restraint, rejoicing in the rare and precious gift they had received together.

"Let's take the day off," Lucas suggested. They were sitting in the kitchen, having just finished breakfast. Duty beckoned, but so did the sun-kissed morning.

"Sounds good," Lorelei said. Sweet languor still filled her. She couldn't imagine marching straight back to the paintbrushes, the speckling and the plastering. They had waited this long, they could wait a little longer.

"Any ideas what you'd like to do?" she asked as they began clearing away the dishes.

He caught her hand, drawing it to his lips. His breath was warm against her skin. Her body tingled, still wrapped in the hazy passion of the night. They had left the bed unmade. She wouldn't have minded returning to it, but Lucas surprised her.

He said, "Let's get out for a while, maybe take a ride up the coast."

She was disappointed, but also a little relieved. Their lovemaking had been so intense that she needed time to regain some semblance of equilibrium. He seemed to sense that, indeed perhaps to share that need.

They headed north along Route 101 into Oregon. To the east, purple shadows drifted over the hills and virgin stands of giant fir. To the west, white-crested waves pounded against beaches alternately golden with sand or dotted with rocks carved by the surf into bridges, arches and lone sentinels standing proud against the vastness just beyond.

The day was crystal clear, the air pleasantly cool. They had taken Lucas's pickup, bumpy but serviceable. There was almost no traffic, sensible folk being at work and the tourist season not yet having started.

Across the state line, near Brookings, they skirted the state park, where wild azaleas abounded. Farther north Lorelei called his attention to the off-shore rocks that, as the tide came in, appeared to resemble spouting whales. Across the soaring bridge over Thomas Creek, they came to Cape Sebastian, the headland rising starkly over the Pacific with views that seemed to go on forever.

There they stopped to stretch their legs. Lorelei was staring out over the water when a sound behind her made her turn. Her face broke into a huge smile when she saw what Lucas was taking from the back of the truck.

"A kite? Where did that come from?"

"My cousin left it there a couple of weeks ago. He was using it with his kids."

"Remember to thank him for me."

Lucas grinned and promised he'd do so. He didn't add, although he did think it, that Sal would be more than surprised when he learned about Lorelei. Like it or not, his life was careering in a direction he could never have foreseen. Princess McGee was suddenly far more than a picture on the cover of *Vogue* or a vague image in his mind. She was a living, breathing, vibrant woman and she was—for better or worse—suddenly very important to him.

He would have said as much to Lorelei, but his instincts told him that he needed to slow down. There was a great deal she didn't know and which he didn't yet feel prepared to tell her. Later, when they were on firmer ground, he could explain about the subterfuge he'd used to get into the house, to get to know her, explain the how and the why. But not now, not while everything was still so new and fragile.

"Want to give it a try?" he asked as he handed her the kite.

"I don't really know how."

He didn't comment on a childhood gone by without acquiring such essential skills as kite flying. Vincent McGee had been a good father in some ways— Lorelei wouldn't be the person she was if he hadn't been. But she'd grown up in a world that, for all its sophistication, lacked a few key elements. Plain, old, unsophisticated fun, for instance.

"Just grab hold and run," he said. "Let the string out as the wind takes it."

Lorelei nodded. She was willing to try. It wasn't as easy as he made out—her first three efforts ended with the kite bumping forlornly along the ground. But on the fourth try, she got it right and the kite sailed skyward.

"Let the string out," Lucas called.

She did so, relishing the tug of the wind on her arms as the kite climbed higher. She could feel the playful strength of the air reaching down through the string to make her feel as though, if she just bounced the right way on her toes, *she* could lift off, rising along with the kite into the cerulean sky.

"This is great!" she yelled as Lucas came up beside her. The tender look of indulgence in his eyes made her forget the kite momentarily, until a good, sharp tug reminded her.

"Up the road a ways on Gold Beach," Lucas said, "I've seen people flying Chinese fighting kites. Those are really incredible."

"I could really get into this," Lorelei said as she watched the kite bob and weave on currents of air. "Next new experience, roller blades."

Lucas winced. "*Please.* I nearly broke my cute you-know-what last year on a pair of those."

Her eyes widened. "What made you try them in the first place?"

"My cousin Sal's kids. They can shame me into anything."

"It sounds as though Sal and you are pretty close."

Lucas hesitated. He had to go carefully here. "He's like a brother to me."

"Any sister?"

"One, but she doesn't live around here."

"What about your parents?" Lorelei asked, her eyes on the kite that was now little more than a dark smudge against the sky.

"They're both dead," he said quietly. "A car accident a few years ago." He didn't add that it had come at a time when he was finally able to provide for them as he would have liked. Sometimes life was just like that.

Lorelei forgot the kite again and looked at him. "I'm sorry."

"That's the way it goes. Anyway, they went together. One of them having to get by without the other would have been tough."

Lorelei tried to imagine what it must have been like to have known two people who were so genuinely in love that they would not have wanted to be parted, even by death. Regretfully she realized that she could not.

The kite climbed higher until almost all the string had run out. They took turns holding onto it, drifting back and forth across the high plateau as the wind drew them. Finally, Lucas drew it down, going carefully as it did belong to Sal's kids and he wouldn't want to be the one to break it. When it was once again safe in the back of the pickup, they walked hand in hand along the edge of the headland, looking out toward the ocean.

"It's been too long since I've done anything like this," Lorelei said quietly.

"Like what?"

"Just taken a day off for no reason and had fun."

"What do you usually do?" Lucas asked. He hadn't thought of her as ever working, but with hindsight he realized that she must. If she lacked the money to bring in a crew to fix up the house, chances were she also had to give at least some thought to putting food on the table.

"I draw," Lorelei said, just a shade defensively. She was used to people who presumed that that meant she dabbled. But the talent, discovered in childhood, had blossomed into a profession that she was proud to have.

"I wish I could," Lucas said, and meant it. It was always a source of amazement to him when someone could pick up a pencil or a pen and, with a handful of lines, create something that looked real. As far as he was concerned, that might as well have been magic. Sal could do it to a certain extent, sketching the interior of a condo or the way landscaping ought to look in at least rough form. And he had people on staff who could do far more, but his own thought processes were strictly three-dimensional; the best way he could show what he was thinking was to build it.

"I'd like to see your work sometime," he said.

"I haven't done anything recently," Lorelei said. "Ever since Dad died, I just haven't wanted to.

But—'' She turned her head, looking all around her at the wild land jutting out into the ocean, the stark blue sky, the man standing next to her.

"I've got a sketch pad in my bag," she said. She always did, the same way a writer kept a notebook or scraps of paper for jotting down ideas, or a photographer kept a camera and film close at hand. "If you don't mind, I'll go get it."

When she returned, Lucas was sitting on a rock watching the play of sunlight on the water. He pointed to a cluster of yellow poppies blooming nearby.

"First of the year," he said.

Lorelei nodded and sat down on a rock. She began to sketch the poppies. He watched unobtrusively. When she flipped the page and began a sketch of the headland, he said, "For some crazy reason, I feel like a nap. If you want to stay for a while, I'm going to stretch out."

She nodded. "By all means, if you're *that* tired."

"Watch it," he warned with a low growl, "I won't always be and then we'll see."

"Promises, promises." But in fact, she didn't begrudge him a rest. They'd had little enough the night before.

While he found a place under a fir tree, she went back to drawing the headland. When that was done, she turned her attention to a group of birds whirling above, catching them in flight across the white paper in quick, dancing lines of charcoal.

She stopped for a few minutes, dusted her fingers off and turned her face to the sun. It was getting on for the afternoon. Lucas was asleep under the tree. She hesitated only briefly before picking up the charcoal again. Working quickly, she drew him as he was, stretched out long and lean, one arm tucked behind his head, eyes closed and features relaxed.

The portrait was as revealing of her as it was of him. Each line, each shadow, bespoke tenderness and something more . . . Something perilously like—

Oh, no, not that. She wasn't in love with him, she couldn't be. They were having a wonderful time together, he made her feel things she'd never felt before, and she wouldn't, for the world, hurt him. But love didn't enter into it.

Her father had loved her mother, foolish though that had been, and he'd ended up alone with a small child to raise. Friends of his, people like Melly and Thad, played at love. They went through life alternately ecstatic and despairing over their relationships. Old-fashioned enough to marry, they divorced with dulling regularity.

And then there were people like Tony, for whom love became the door to despair and life itself became unbearable.

No, thank you very much, she was *not* in love. Not anything like it. No way, no how, no sirree.

Her throat dry, she stared at the sketch in her lap. It was good but, heaven help her, it was only a pale reflection of the man himself.

He stirred, and she shut the sketch pad hastily. By the time he had risen and started toward her, she had her smile firmly in place, masking the piercing shock of awareness as she realized just where her feelings for him were heading.

Eight

"I need to stop at my place to pick up a few things," Lucas said as they were heading back.

Beside him, Lorelei nodded. They didn't discuss the fact that he would once again spend the night, they didn't need to.

A little shiver of apprehension moved through her as she thought how she would feel if he suddenly hadn't wanted to stay. She was vulnerable in a way she had never before known.

Part of her actually rejoiced at that, for she felt so much more alive, so enriched by what she shared with Lucas. Yet there was no getting away from the truth. After a lifetime spent safe within the strangely cosseting world of her father and his friends, when her only venture into trouble had seen her rescued by a man who'd wanted nothing from her but gentleness and companionship, she was at last free to give herself fully, without hindrance, with all the risks that implied.

And she would not have had it otherwise.

Lucas was mostly silent after they crossed the state line and continued south. He seemed preoccupied by his own thoughts.

That suited Lorelei. She was content to tilt her head back against the seat, close her eyes and let her spirit drift with the swiftly passing miles.

But all too soon they pulled up in front of a low, sun-washed wooden fence set within sight of the ocean on a small rise outside of town. Beyond the fence was a cluster of unpretentious houses that vaguely reminded her of the structures fishermen and other settlers had built when they first came to the northwest. They were similar in some ways to the clapboard saltboxes of New England, yet had a uniqueness all their own.

"You live here?" she asked, not without a little surprise. If the houses, and the cars parked in front of them, were anything to go by, the area was rather more affluent than one would expect of an itinerant handyman.

"I bummed around the country some," Lucas said, "had a bunch of jobs and did pretty well. I'm kind of taking it easy now that I'm back."

Strictly speaking it was true, but only strictly. He *had* lived in many parts of the country and worked a lot of jobs, only they had all involved construction and in recent years had been for his own company. And he had, by his own definition, been on a more relaxed schedule since returning to San Cristobal, although it was doubtful anyone else would look at his hours and see it that way.

"I can wait here if you like," Lorelei suggested as he parked in front of one of the units near the entrance to the complex. She'd sensed a sudden reticence in Lucas and the last thing she wanted to do was invade his privacy.

She smiled slightly at that, thinking it a strange thought, given the intimacy between them. But there were all kinds and levels of intimacy, and sometimes the simplest things could be the most complex.

For just an instant, though, she thought her guess had been right, and Lucas really didn't want her to go in with him. But the thought was gone almost as rapidly as the odd look disappeared from his eyes.

Smiling, he said, "You'd rather come in, wouldn't you? It's been a long drive and I ought to have something cold in the fridge."

Lorelei agreed that sounded good and followed him up the stone steps, which were surrounded by small, neatly clipped juniper bushes. The clapboard was stained a shade of gray-blue that reminded her of deep, cool water. The windows wore white shutters. All very homey yet elegant. She was trying hard to keep her curiosity under wraps, but didn't quite succeed. A sudden need to know more about him made her step with more than her usual swiftness into the house.

Her first reaction was one of bewilderment. Cunning little dried-flower arrangements in driftwood on a glass and brass hall table? Chintz pillows on a couch glimpsed through the arch that led to what must be the living room? A lithograph of mist enfolding rocks where seal mothers looked after their pups?

None of it, absolutely none, tallied with the man she thought she was getting to know. He was many things, but predictable wasn't one of them.

"It's...uh...very nice," she said, glancing around the spacious, two-story entry, while trying not to knit her brow in consternation.

"The decorator liked it," Lucas muttered absently. The light on his answering machine, just visible on the kitchen counter, was blinking. He should have checked in before, but he'd been busy. Very, very busy.

"Decorator?" Lorelei repeated. That didn't make any sense, either. Okay, he'd done "pretty well" on the jobs he'd had while "bumming around," but enough to both buy this place *and* hire a decorator?

"This unit was the model," he explained, seeing her surprise, "when the complex was being sold. It's the last one left. I'm baby-sitting it, I guess you could say."

Lorelei's eyes cleared. Her face relaxed into a smile. "Oh, I see. For a friend?"

"You could say that." Hey, if a guy couldn't be his own friend, who could be?

"It really is nice," she said, sincerely this time.

"It's okay. Most places like this end up looking the same, like they were furnished straight out of some magazine that describes how people are supposed to live but never do. I mean, seriously, look at this stuff. Who in his right mind would have this stuff around? You have to dust it, or hire somebody else to do it. One wrong move and something breaks. And heaven forbid you have a dog or worse yet, a few kids. Then the whole place looks like a wreck in no time."

"It sounds like you've been giving this some thought," Lorelei said, puzzled again. It didn't seem like the kind of thing he'd be concerned about.

"As a matter of fact, I have," Lucas admitted. He had even gone so far as to establish a new policy for the models in his complexes. They were now decorated to look as though somebody was actually living in them—the day's newspaper left out on a table, food in the kitchen—with lots of emphasis on easy care. Women, in particular, seemed to be responding to the last part.

He offered no further explanation for his interest, but said, "Why don't you help yourself to a drink while I get a few things together?"

She agreed, feeling suddenly self-conscious. Lucas seemed to sense that and, smiling gently, dropped a quick kiss on her mouth. At least, it was meant to be quick. But barely had it begun than the kiss deepened and passion turned hot and fierce.

A day's abstinence had made their need for each other only greater. Lorelei was hardly aware when he carried her into the bedroom and laid her down on a large platform bed. She was conscious of little else but the touch and feel of his hard, powerful body along every inch of her own.

Fumbling in their haste, they removed each other's clothes. When his chest was bare, Lorelei pressed her lips against him, over his flat male nipples, the furls of dark hair arrowing down toward his abdomen, the hard ridge of muscles across his ribs. On and on until he made a harsh sound deep in his throat and his hands closed on her shoulders.

Pressing her into the mattress, he parted her legs, stroking her thighs, opening her, readying her, until she cried out his name and drew him to her.

For long, incandescent moments they moved as one, passion thrusting them higher and higher, until the world exploded into shards of light and for one brief, blissful moment only they existed.

Slowly, reluctantly, consciousness re-formed. Lorelei found herself lying on her side, her head resting on Lucas's broad shoulder, her hair spread out over his chest. His breathing was still ragged, but his smile was replete with male satisfaction.

"Beats aerobics any day," he said.

"Beats anything any day," she corrected teasingly.

He nodded, his gaze suddenly serious. "That's the truth. You flat out amaze me, Miss Lorelei McGee."

"It's mutual," she said softly.

They lay in silence for a time until the chiming of the clock in the living room reminded them that time was passing. Outside, the light was fading, giving way to the softness of early evening.

"I don't know about you," Lucas said, "but I'm starved."

"What's in the fridge?"

"A six-pack of beer and some liverwurst that's been with me so long I don't have the heart to get rid of it."

"We can eat at my place," she said hastily.

"Better yet, let's go out." He kissed her lightly and stood up. "I'll get what I need together."

"You do that," Lorelei murmured, wondering where all that business came from about men being depleted after lovemaking. He looked like he'd been for a nice, invigorating jog, while she was still lying there trying to figure out how to get her knees to work again.

Not that she was complaining. Not at all.

Half an hour later, having finally managed to get up and having located most of her clothes—the bra had to be someplace, she just couldn't find it—she joined Lucas in the kitchen. He was dumping water on what looked like a long-suffering ivy plant.

"Also courtesy of the decorator?" Lorelei asked.

He nodded. "Everything except the clothes and most of the books. I like to travel light."

It was on the tip of her tongue to ask him how long he was thinking of sticking around this time, but she

couldn't bring herself to do it. She had a feeling she
wouldn't like the answer.

They went back to her house, dropped off Lucas's gear and then headed south for a place he described as down-home, no fuss, no muss. It turned
out to be a little bit more.

Sherree's Good Time Café was one of those places
Lorelei had vaguely heard of but had never been
near. It was about thirty miles outside the San Cristobal and attracted a crowd that was part tourist,
part local and part your-guess-is-as-good-as-mine.

Located in a defunct service station that had been
only minimally redecorated, the café opened at 5:00
p.m. and closed precisely twelve hours later, no
matter what was still going on. Sherree being absolutely determined that everybody get a good rest,
spend some time with their family and show up at
work more or less when they were supposed to.

Lucas was just a little bit in love with Sherree, but
then, so were most of the men who showed up there
once a day or once a week or once a decade. She was
a hundred pounds wringing wet of no-nonsense,
we're-all-in-this-together cheerfulness, and there
weren't too many like her.

She also served up some of the best cooking to be
found anywhere, consisting of whatever was fresh in

the market that day and used in recipes her momma had taught her and her momma before her.

"Sherree's about two-hundred years old," Lucas said, "give or take a decade. At least, she seems that way. I don't suppose there's anything left that could surprise her."

He was wrong. The sight of Lucas Messina walking into her place with a lady he looked—she could tell at one glance—serious about—that was serious with a capital S—now that was something Sherree just couldn't remember seeing before, not once, in all the long, off-again, on-again years she had known him.

But she had enough sense—being famous for it—to keep her mouth shut and let him do the talking.

"Hey, Sherree," said Lucas. "This is a friend of mine, Lorelei McGee. Lorelei, say hi to Sherree."

"Hi," Lorelei said, a bit bemusedly, but then Sherree didn't blame her for that. She wouldn't blame any woman for feeling that way after finding herself on the arm of the six-foot-plus, bold-as-brass masculinity that was Lucas Messina.

Fact was, had Sherree been a tad younger—by several decades—she might have been tempted to give Lorelei a run for her money. As it was, she just stood off to one side and enjoyed.

"Nice to meet you, Miss McGee," Sherree said, very properlike. She smoothed her platinum blond hair, gave a little hitch to her purple spandex leggings, and gestured to a table right next to the dance floor.

"What's good tonight?" Lucas asked when they were seated.

Sherree put her hands on her hips and looked down at him from her full five-feet-nothing. "Now, when have I ever dished up something that wasn't?"

Lucas laughed. Sherree had a funny way of making time feel like it was rolling back. He could have been nineteen years old again, still wet behind the ears and mad at most of the world for the careless injustices it inflicted.

Except that he wasn't. He could sit and remember what it had felt like to be nineteen and take some pardonable satisfaction in just how much things had changed.

"There was the time with the possum," he said.

"Hush your mouth. I told you that was no possum, it was plain old razorback and it was supposed to be a joke."

"Your story. Tasted like possum."

"How would you know? Where you been that you'd even have a chance to eat possum? Filet mignon, maybe, but not pos—" She caught herself, flushed and closed her mouth with a snap. Lucas had a way of not wanting himself talked about, which Sherree understood, being partial to her own privacy, too.

"You'd be surprised," Lucas said softly. He appreciated her discretion even if it did come a little late.

"What I meant," Sherree said, more to Lorelei than to Lucas, "was that he always did know quality. Nothing wrong with that, is there?"

"Not that I can think of," Lorelei agreed. There was something going on here that had her ears prickling, but she wasn't sure what it might be. Lucas was looking a little nervous, unusual for him, as though he thought Sherree might blurt out something he'd rather not have said.

But what she did say was, "Brunswick stew's on the menu, along with sourdough rolls, some real nice smoked ham and a cress salad straight out of the greenhouse. How does that sound?"

"Too good to pass up," Lucas said. "What do you think?" he asked Lorelei.

She put her menu down without bothering to look at it and smiled. "Perfect."

Sherree nodded, gave them both one last quick once-over, and then made herself scarce.

"So what do you think?" Lucas asked, looking across the table.

Lorelei hesitated. She picked up a fork, twirled it a few times and put it down again. "About what?"

He was wearing a plain white shirt that was frayed at the collar and cuffs. It looked as if it had been used for business at some point and kept around for more casual wear. The fabric strained slightly when his big, muscular shoulders—which she remembered with such crystal clarity—moved up and down.

"About this place, life in general, us."

"Interesting, interesting and—interesting."

He laughed ruefully. "A woman of few words."

"Oh, I don't know about that. I could say something about how my whole life has been turned upside down in the past twenty-four hours. About how I don't know if I'm coming or going and I don't much care, and about how I'm not really sure of who you are or why you make me feel the way I do. But I won't. Because I only know that the past twenty-four hours are the best thing that's happened to me in a long time."

She ended on a note of such gentleness that Lucas found he had to look away for just a second, because if he didn't he might be tempted to say something about who he really was, to reveal the truth that he wasn't yet ready to, even though he damn well knew that he ought to.

But there was another truth stopping him and that was that he, Lucas Messina, who had never been afraid of anything in his life, was suddenly, desperately, stomach-churningly afraid of losing the beautiful, vulnerable woman sitting across the table from him.

Go figure that one, he thought, and stood up.

"Let's dance."

They did, slow and easy, to the strains of original music from the sixties and seventies, with even a little fifties and forties thrown in, their bodies swaying back and forth, maybe a little closer than they ought to have been for the sake of sanity, but what the heck, the night was young.

They returned to the table just when the Brunswick stew got there. It was as good as Sherree had promised, as was everything else. They were both hungry and did justice to the meal.

In the end they danced more than they talked, sometimes just sitting, holding hands across the table and looking at each other the way couples did in the old movies, as if the world had narrowed in some remarkable way to just one another.

Lucas had never believed that was actually possible. He was finding out differently.

But he was also walking a tightrope, because, sooner or later—and if he had any sense at all, it had to be sooner—he was going to have to level with Miss Lorelei McGee.

And heaven help him when he did.

Nine

Much later that night, Lucas remembered that he'd meant to check in with his answering machine. Why exactly he would come out of a deep, satiated sleep to remember any such thing, he couldn't say, but it undoubtedly had something to do with an overly conscientious nature.

Leaving Lorelei's bed, he walked quietly from the room and made his way downstairs to the kitchen. He dialed the number, waited and then used the remote code to trigger the tape.

What he heard banished the sweet afterglow of contentment as effectively as a cold shower.

"Bad news, boss," Lisa's voice said over the line, "we've got a problem at Mountain Falls. Remember all the questions you had during development about the nature preserve next door? You wanted to make sure it was as pristine as it sounded? I hate to tell you, but the local paper's about to break the news that the place was used as an illegal dump—ten, fifteen years ago. Sorry to drop this on you, but there's no easy way to say it. Let me know how you want it handled."

The message ended, the tape whirled and Lisa was back.

"Sorry to bother you again, but I thought you'd call in by now. The Mountain Falls problem is for sure, the local paper is running with the story tomorrow. They want a comment from us. Anything?"

And then a third time. "I'm getting nervous not hearing from you. Hope you don't mind, but I'm calling Sal. Check in when you can."

Damn it, Lucas thought. His fist hit the counter. Damn it to hell. Just what he didn't need, a major problem with a development and him being out of touch. Lisa had been right to call Sal, but knowing that didn't make him feel any better. It was *his* company, *his* responsibility and he should have been there when he was needed instead of—

No regrets, his mind said. No matter what, he simply couldn't muster them. His thoughts went to Lorelei, asleep upstairs, and he managed a faint smile. If he had to be distracted, at least he had a damn good reason.

But he had to put that aside for now and respond to the emergency facing his company. The Mountain Falls project could be completely destroyed by this news. The remaining twenty percent of the units, which effectively represented his profit, would go unsold and those buyers who were already in would be clamoring to get out.

Worse yet, if there was anything to the illegal dump story, he'd have to buy them out even if it left him broke. Too many of those people had kids, and there were couples who were planning on having more. He couldn't possibly leave them in danger.

He found a piece of paper, scrawled a message for Lorelei and took it back upstairs. He dressed in the dark, never taking his eyes from her, and left the message on the pillow where, just a short time before, his head had lain. She'd see it as soon as she woke.

He bent down and dropped a light kiss on her brow. She stirred slightly and reached out a hand toward him. He took it but only long enough to slip it back under the covers.

Walking out of that room, away from her, was one of the hardest things he'd ever done in his life. But he had no choice. Too many people were counting on him.

Driving through the darkness, he reached Mountain Falls by early morning. By then, he'd talked with Sal on the car phone and agreed that their initial response should be calm but decisive. He needed to see the information the paper was basing their story on and he needed to see it fast.

Which was why he was sitting in his car outside the office of the Mountain Falls *Gazette,* sipping a cup of coffee from the Delite Donut Shop down the street and watching the clock on the dashboard crawl toward 8:00 a.m., when the *Gazette's* offices would open.

Lucas was finishing his coffee just about the time Lorelei woke up. And he was getting out of the car and heading for the *Gazette* when she opened her eyes, found the bed empty beside her and saw the note.

"Have to leave on business. Back soon. Lucas."

She blinked, read it again and frowned. She wasn't a morning person, one of those unfortunate individuals who bounded from sleep with a song on their lips, eager to jump into the new day. She preferred to ease into it—slowly. Her heart didn't even really start beating until she'd had a cup of coffee, and she saw no reason to rush it.

Which was why it took a few minutes for the note to sink in.

Still holding it, she got out of bed, padded into the bathroom, set the note down on the counter next to the sink and kept one eye on it as she brushed her teeth.

It didn't go away. Teeth brushed, hair brushed, she picked it up and read it again.

Leave... business... back... Lucas.

Not exactly a fount of information. Or for that matter, affection. Nothing there to indicate the slightest degree of intimacy. He could have been leaving a note for the milkman.

Her frown deepened. She felt suddenly cold, enough so that she went back into the bedroom and dressed hastily, pulling jeans and a sweater from the closet without really noticing what she was putting on.

By the time she was done, she had a better grip on herself. It would be crazy to read too much into this.

She'd sensed all along that there was more to Lucas than he necessarily revealed, and she'd chosen to become involved with him despite that. She couldn't claim now to be too upset if she didn't like some of the results.

The smartest thing she could do now was to keep herself busy, but that presented some problems. To begin with, she was almost out of paint again. And while the second floor of the house looked much better than it had even a short time before, it still needed a lot of work. The sooner she got on with it, the better.

She made a quick list of what she needed, checked it over and headed for her car.

The paint store was at the far end of San Cristobal's main street, in a mini-mall that included a supermarket, a video store, a boutique and a few other odds-and-ends-type stores. Lorelei parked and got out without taking much notice of her surroundings. Like it or not, she was still thinking about Lucas.

Or at least she was until a well-dressed man of medium height with a mile-wide smile intercepted her path.

"Miss McGee," he said. "It *is* Lorelei McGee, isn't it? Vincent McGee's daughter?"

Instinctively, Lorelei drew back. She glanced at him quickly, looked away and kept going. "Excuse me."

"Hey, wait a sec," he said as he trotted to keep up with her. "You're just the person I've been hoping to run into, Miss McGee. I'm Jason Brandeis from the *Inquisitor.*"

Lorelei quickened her step. She said nothing, hoping that her icy silence would be her best defense. Besides, it was the only sensible course of action. Anything she said—anything at all—could, she knew, be twisted until it was unrecognizable.

"Something tells me that doesn't thrill you," Brandeis said with a chuckle. "But, hey, that's all right. I've gotten the bum's rush from experts."

His cheerfulness in the face of her obvious disinclination to talk surprised Lorelei. She slowed down slightly but still said nothing.

"It's no skin off my nose," he went on. "Fact is, I've given up trying to get an interview with you. The Big Guy took care of that."

"Big Guy—" she said, despite herself. "You mean—"

"Hey, I think it's really great that the two of you got together. Lucas Messina and Vincent McGee's little girl, imagine that. Just goes to show anything's possible." His smile broadened.

Lorelei took a deep breath. The impulse to tell Jason Brandeis to go take a long hike off a short pier was very strong. On the other hand, the bait he dangled was pretty nigh irresistible.

"All right," she said reluctantly. Stopping right where she was, on the sidewalk in front of the paint store, she looked him square in the eye. "Suppose you tell me what this is all about."

Brandeis did a long, slow double take, as if she'd surprised him. "About? It's not about anything. All I'm saying is that I think it's real nice. Letting bygones be bygones and all that."

Lorelei folded her arms in front of her, straightened her shoulders and summoned all her patience. "Thirty seconds, Mr. Brandeis, that's it."

He sighed, ran a hand through his hair, and blurted, "Lucas Messina is the grandson and grandnephew of the men who built your father's house. The scuttlebutt is that they were never fully paid for the job, this despite the fact that one of them had an accident that killed him. The family's hopes for the future were destroyed, they were plunged into poverty, et cetera, et cetera."

Lorelei paled. A wave of coldness roared through her. She looked at him in disbelief. "What are you talking about? My father never cheated anyone. He always—"

"Your faith in him is real touching," Brandeis interrupted. He eyed her assessingly. Too late, she realized that she had given him exactly the reaction he had hoped for. He had a story now, namely that she hadn't known who Lucas really was or what linked him to her father's house. By ordinary news standards, it wasn't much, but the *Inquisitor* could turn it into page-one material.

"I'm just telling you what people say," Brandeis went on smoothly. He spread his heads as though he thought it was really too bad and sympathized with her, when he, of course, did anything but.

"But, hey," he went on, "that's all in the past. Messìna Construction is riding high now. Thanks to the Big Guy—who is one hell of a tough business-man—they've got some of the most successful resi-dential projects in the country. It's only natural that he'd want to celebrate his climb to the top by mov-ing into the house his family built, right?"

Lorelei's mouth thinned. With a grip on her emo-tions that was so tight it hurt, she said, "Goodbye, Mr. Brandeis."

She made to brush past him, but his hand lashed out, fastening on her arm. Lorelei stopped dead and stared pointedly. Her voice was ice-edged as she said, "Let go of me."

Brandeis pulled his hand back as though it had been burned. He stared at her warily. It wasn't her he was scared of, she was sure of that. But something had spooked him. Grimly she realized it must be Lucas—the Big Guy—he was afraid of offending, not her.

"Sorry," he said hastily. "I wasn't thinking. Look, whatever's going on, nobody's going to blame you for it. But our readers *would* appreciate knowing how you and Lucas found each other. It's kind of a Romeo and Juliet story, you know?"

Lorelei closed her eyes for a moment against the wave of revulsion she felt. Not against Brandeis, there was no point in that, but against the whole tawdry, cruel mess. How could she have been such a fool? All her life, she had seen people using and being used by others. Why would she have thought it would be any different with Lucas? He wanted the house—and possibly revenge. Not her.

Her eyes burned and she wanted very much to cry, but there was no power on earth that could make her give in to the urge. Not even Lucas Messina.

"Goodbye, Mr. Brandeis," she said again, and this time she meant it. The door to the paint store shut in his face.

Ten minutes later, Lorelei came out, minus any paint. She had simply stood inside the store, hoping no one would try to talk to her, until she was sure Brandeis was gone.

Once the coast was clear, she got into her car, but she made no effort to leave the parking lot. Instead she sat behind the wheel and forced herself to think.

Messina Construction, Brandeis had said. Riding high. So much for the itinerant handyman routine, *if* Brandeis was telling the truth. Or anything that remotely resembled it.

Lucas lived in San Cristobal, she had seen that for herself. If he did own such a business, it had to be located somewhere in the immediate area. She had never heard of a Messina Construction company, nor had her father ever mentioned it. There was at least a chance that it didn't exist except in Jason Brandeis's fevered imagination.

Buoyed by the thought, she got out of the car and went over to a public phone booth not far from where she was parked. When she asked the information operator for the number for Messina Construction, she hoped to hear that there was none. Instead a series of recorded digits spewed into her ear.

Ordinarily, Lorelei was no better at remembering numbers than were most people, but these instantly etched themselves into her memory. She hung up, waited a moment and lifted the receiver again.

Moments later, a cool, elegant voice said, "Messina Construction. May I help you?"

"I need your address," Lorelei said. Distantly, as though she was standing apart from herself, she marveled at how she managed to sound as if she had no greater interest than to send a letter.

Lorelei thanked the woman and then hung up. She forced herself to walk back to the car, get in and turn the key.

Ten minutes later she was sitting in front of the headquarters of Messina Construction. It was a low building, elegantly made of glass and black steel, surrounded by sumptuous landscaping. A fountain played out in front. There was a guard post at the entrance to the parking lot, manned by a security guard, who eyed her discreetly.

Lorelei parked the car, but sat where she was, hands frozen on the wheel. Messina Construction existed and if appearances were anything to go by, Lucas was a very successful and wealthy man.

Brandeis had been right about that much, at least. Much as she wanted to believe he'd been wrong about the rest, she couldn't manage it.

She was starting to feel foolish sitting there, and beginning to think that she really had to leave, when she saw a large, dark-haired man hurrying toward the building. He bore a passing resemblance to Lucas, although he lacked his rugged build and compelling manner.

On impulse, she got out of the car and approached him.

"Excuse me," she said, "I'm looking for Lucas Messina. Do you know if he's here?"

The man looked at her blankly for a moment before he shook his head. "He's out of town. If you want, you can leave a message with his secretary."

That said, Sal hurried on. Ordinarily he would have at least been curious about who the young woman was and what she had to do with his cousin. But he was too busy worrying about Mountain Falls to think about anything else. By the time he had reached his office, he had forgotten all about the encounter.

Lisa was also extremely preoccupied that morning. Enough so that when a woman called to say that she needed to get in touch with Lucas, Lisa automatically gave her the number where he'd said he could be reached.

It took Lorelei only a few minutes to determine that the number belonged to a motel outside of someplace called Mountain Falls, about a hundred miles down the coast. She hesitated only briefly before deciding what she had to do.

Ten

Lorelei went back to the house, made herself a cup of tea and determinedly set about going through her father's financial records. She had made some progress earlier, but a great deal had been put on hold while she concentrated on the house—and on Lucas. Now it couldn't wait.

The task was daunting. Over the years Vincent had kept a bewildering array of material, all of it vaguely financial, but none of it remotely organized.

She found some tax returns, but there were also years for which there were none, or at least none she could lay her hands on. There were contracts for movies he'd done, canceled checks, deposit receipts, restaurant bills, even numbers scrawled on matchbooks and napkins that seemed to be related to deals he'd been involved with.

Several hours into the job, she was headachy, weary and no closer to what she needed to find. And her search had raised so much dust in the den that she finally couldn't stand it any longer and dragged the boxes into the living room.

Determined to impose some sense of order, she began sorting the material into piles by year. The most recent piles were small; her father's financial dealings had sunk to almost nothing. But for his productive years the piles grew larger and larger.

From scattered notes she found, she concluded that at one time or another most of the material had been in the hands of various agents or financial managers. She found letters from no fewer than four of them, detailing various arrangements, and their signatures appeared on several documents. But nowhere could she find a single general accounting of her father's finances for any period of his life. Apparently none of the people responsible for taking care of his money had considered it necessary to tell him what they were doing with it.

At last, she found the cartons that held material for the years when the house was being built. Before delving into them, she took a short break, made herself another cup of tea and went out on the terrace for a few minutes to get some fresh air.

In the back of her mind, she was afraid of what she would find. If Brandeis was right—

But there was no point standing around worrying about it. What was, was, and she would have to deal with it.

Back in the living room, she sat cross-legged on the floor and began going through the cartons. She found the early plans for the house, the refinements added to them and finally the actual blueprints. There was also the deed for the land, records of payments made to various suppliers for materials and a letter to the builders, addressed to Dominique and Paul . . . Messina.

Her hand shook as she read it over. The letter was straightforward in the extreme. Vincent simply confirmed that he agreed to their terms and wanted them to begin work immediately. But Lorelei suspected the wording wasn't his, that he had merely signed it. Which seemed to be confirmed by a postscript that directed that any questions be forwarded to his business manager, as Vincent himself would be tied up on a new movie.

She wondered absently which one it had been as she delved into the carton again. Try though she did, she couldn't find an actual contract between her father and the Messina brothers. They seemed to have conducted their business very informally.

But perhaps that wasn't so surprising. Back then, people hadn't been as concerned with legalities as they were now. And a man's word had still been seriously considered to be his bond.

Or at least it had been in most quarters.

The tea and the aspirin she'd taken were no longer enough to hold off the headache that had been threatening all day. Reluctantly she gave the piles of paper a final glance, stood up and left the living room.

Climbing the stairs to bed, she struggled not to think of how different this night was from the previous one. Then Lucas had been here, shattering her solitude, claiming her as his own and at the same time giving of himself with such breathtaking generosity that she still, even now, could not fully bring herself to believe that he had deceived her.

Yet try as she might to prove otherwise, she had to admit that everything Brandeis had told her was proving true. Lucas's family had built the house and there was evidence to suggest that they hadn't been very well protected legally when they did so. Her father's financial affairs had never been well organized, raising at least the possibility that payments that should have been made might not have been.

And Messina Construction did exist. It was, by all appearances, a highly successful business founded by a man who hadn't let any hardship hold him back from what he wanted in life.

Brandeis said Lucas wanted the house.

Lorelei wanted to believe that he wanted her. But the legacy of a lifetime—seeing people treated like objects and ultimately discarded—eroded her confidence and mocked her dreams.

She went to bed uneasily, slept poorly and woke to find her pillow wet with tears.

Lucas didn't sleep at all. He'd taken over one of the unsold units at the Mountain Falls development, and he spent the night sitting there, drinking cup after cup of coffee and trying to figure out how to salvage what he had spent a lifetime building.

The *Gazette*'s editor had proved singularly unhelpful. They were going with the story, plain and simple. He was sorry, but he had a duty to inform the public.

No, he wouldn't tell Lucas who his source was for the information. The source had asked for anonymity and it was the editor's job to give it. That struck Lucas as a singularly convenient position, one that would allow any lie or distortion to be presented as fact. But the editor saw it differently and he wasn't giving an inch.

Come morning, when the paper hit the stands, all hell was going to break loose.

To make matters worse, as desperately as he had to concentrate on the situation at hand, his thoughts kept wandering to Lorelei. He had left her so abruptly. What was she thinking? Did she wonder at all where he'd gone? Did she miss him?

He made a sound of disgust deep in his throat and got up so abruptly that the chair he'd been sitting in tumbled backward, landing with a crash. Lucas righted it, walked over to the sink, walked back again—

Oh, great, now he was pacing. In the midst of the worst crisis he'd ever faced, with his business hanging by a thread, all he could think of was a certain mahogany-haired enchantress with crystalline blue eyes, a body that didn't stop and more sweet, generous passion than he'd ever even dreamed of.

Never mind the coffin in the living room and the severed heads in the kitchen cupboard—and especially never mind whatever it was that was down in the basement. Lorelei McGee had gotten under his skin in a way he'd never thought possible.

He ought to call her, tell her what was going on. Except to do that, he'd have to explain. And if he did, he risked losing her. Risked having her turn on him for deliberately deceiving her about his identity and his motives. With everything else that was going on, he just couldn't face that right now.

He went to bed finally and even slept for a few hours, waking to a gray morning wrapped in fog.

Lucas stood up slowly and let the soil trickle through his fingers. It was good earth, rich, dark and loamy, the kind his grandfather had always liked best for growing grapes. Given the slightest chance, it would bring forth life in profusion.

As it had here in the nature preserve, next to where he had built. He was surrounded by trees and shrubs now coming into leaf and beginning to bloom. Birds were singing and he could hear the scampering of small animals along the forest floor. The very air itself was filled with the scents of living things.

And yet, if the reports were to be believed, there was death here, too. He couldn't accept that, but he couldn't ignore it, either. A small stream ran near where he was standing. On impulse, he bent down, cupped his hand and caught a splash of the water. It tasted sweet and pure.

He moved on, closer now to the borders of the development. He had deliberately left a broad swath of untouched land between the housing and the preserve, not because he was required to do so, but because he hadn't wanted to create the impression of a sudden, sharp break. Instead, the preserve and the development seemed to blend into one another. The trees gave way only gradually. Instead of the usual chemically induced lawns, a meadow emerged from the forest, bright with the year's first wildflowers. Standing quietly on the edge of it, Lucas watched a doe and her fawn glide by serenely.

He was proud of Mountain Falls. Yes, he stood to make a substantial profit when all the units were sold, but he could have made far more had he been willing to exploit the land without thought or restraint. The idea that someone else had done so, and in the process endangered dozens of men, women and children, infuriated him.

His eyes were hard as he walked back toward the development.

They were harder still when he saw the bright red paint splashed on the front door of the unit he was using. He stood, hands on his hips, staring at the vandalism. It was totally unjustified, but not unexpected. People had put their life savings into Mountain Falls. They were frightened, angry and not too far from panic. Something had to change fast.

Avoiding the still-wet paint, he went inside. Minutes later he had unpacked his "notebook" computer, dialed the office and gained access to the files on the Mountain Falls project.

Eleven

Lorelei pulled the last of the weeds from the flower bed where she had been working, straightened up and arched her neck. She'd been at it since before dawn, working nonstop, exactly as she had for the past three days. All in a futile effort to put Lucas out of her mind.

Not that it was a total waste. She had finished painting the second-floor rooms, organized her father's financial records as far as anyone possibly could, scoured all the kitchen cabinets—which also involved getting rid of the head collection—and had even replastered a section of the ceiling in the front hall.

Who said she needed help?

It was amazing what she could accomplish when fueled by a potent mixture of anger, bewilderment, uncertainty and plain old fear.

Damn the man!

He'd had no right to come waltzing into her life, turn it upside down and then blithely disappear, leaving her to deal with the wreckage.

Although, to be truthful, disappear wasn't really the right word. She knew where he was. Therein lay the problem.

For the past three days she had fought the temptation to go after him. Purely to give him a piece of her mind, of course. He had lied to her, misled her, made her hope and dream as she never had before, and worse yet, left her to find out the truth from a man who, on a good day, made her want to run in the opposite direction.

All in all, not the basis for a lasting relationship.

And yet, some inner part of her insisted on going its own way, stubbornly recalling all Lucas's good points, his patience and gentleness, his tender passion and care, how he made her feel more alive than she ever had before.

There were also the dreams from which she woke trembling, filled with yearning, reaching out to him. Dreams that made sleep a battleground and drove her from her bed while the world lay wrapped in stillness.

But not now. The sun was up, the sky was clear, and the healthy tiredness of her body made her efforts worthwhile. She would keep working throughout the day and tonight she would sleep without dreams, whole and sufficient by herself.

Sure she would.

The worst part was how casually he had left her, without a word of explanation. Knowing where he had gone wasn't enough. As the days crept by, she slowly admitted that what she really needed to know was why he had gone.

Anything was better than deluding herself, pretending that he cared about her when in fact he did not. Better to be hurt, no matter how badly, than to go on being a fool.

Of course, she could simply wait and confront him when he returned. But as the days passed and he didn't return, she was losing her taste for dignified restraint. It was costing her too much emotionally.

She went back into the house, poured herself a glass of iced tea and carried it out to the gazebo. She had avoided the small structure since Lucas's depar-

ture, but now she forced herself to enter it. There
were so many memories there, recent ones that she
shied away from, but also many others dating back
throughout her childhood.

Her face softened as she thought about the person she had been, the quiet and serious child with her
nose in a book or lost in a daydream. A child who'd
grown up among adults inhabiting a glamorous fan-
tasy world.

Early on she had acquired a certain sophistication
that was no more a part of her true self than some
outfit she might have borrowed from Aunt Melly.
But the disguise had been useful, enabling her to
move through her world without ever really revealing or committing herself.

Always protected—by her father, by Tony, even by
Thad and Melly and others like them—beautiful
Princess McGee, not quite real, a figure of specula-
tion and rumor, always just out of reach of everyone, including herself.

Except that wasn't who she was. She was a real,
honest-to-God woman, who lived and breathed
and—heaven help her—loved. And right now she
hurt, terribly, constantly, with an aching emptiness
deep inside that was growing worse by the moment.

The glass slipped from her hand. She watched almost absently as it smashed into dozens of tiny frag-

ments on the floor of the gazebo. The tea spread in a brown stain over the wood and dripped away onto the ground below.

Abruptly she stood up and walked toward the house.

Lucas had finally finished going over the environmental studies on the Mountain Falls project. His recollection of them had been correct—they'd been thorough to the point of being exhaustive and they had turned up nothing, absolutely nothing that could indicate toxic waste dumping had taken place anywhere in or near the development site. If toxic wastes were present, they had been dumped since construction finished.

Grimly he snapped off the computer and sat back. He had already ordered up new studies, but they would take weeks to finish and in the meantime, the residents weren't willing to simply wait. Not if the meeting he'd had that morning was anything to go by.

Already there was talk of legal action that could effectively deny him permits to build anywhere in the state. His business would be at a standstill until he could prove he had done nothing wrong.

The injustice of that ate at him, but he refused to give in to it. Life was what life was; he'd been dealing with it long enough to know that.

He was considering his next move when the door-bell rang. Cautiously, Lucas got up to answer it. The last thing he needed now was more trouble. Prepared to deal quickly and, if necessary, roughly with whoever might be standing there, he was utterly unprepared for what greeted his eyes.

Lorelei stared at the red stain disfiguring the door. A breeze ruffled her mahogany hair. Her cheeks were slightly flushed. She looked cool, beautiful and unbearably desirable.

"If I were you," she said, regarding the stain, "I'd get back in touch with that decorator."

Lucas shook his head once in a futile effort to clear it. He stood aside. "Come in." Even to his own ears, his voice sounded thick.

He had managed until that very moment to keep his hunger for her in check, even to partially deny it. But to see her like this, without any warning, suddenly appearing in the midst of all his worry and anger, was like an unexpected gift, one he couldn't honestly say he deserved.

But neither was he about to turn it away. At least not until he knew for certain why she had come.

She walked into the house, glanced around and turned to look at him.

"Don't you think you should close the door?" she asked.

Belatedly realizing that he was standing there with his hand on the doorknob, he let the door shut. His mouth was suddenly dry.

"I don't suppose your being here is sheer coincidence?" he asked.

She shook her head. "'Fraid not. I ran into Brandeis."

Cautiously, his stomach clenching, he asked, "So?"

"So when he couldn't get to me, he got interested in you. Naturally, I didn't take anything he said as gospel, but for once he really was telling the truth."

His face tightened. Regret filled him. He should have been honest with her, should have taken the risk and told her the truth rather than leave her to find it out for herself. Especially through Brandeis, of all people!

But he hadn't done that and there was no going back. For all her attempt at calmness, he could see the pain in her eyes and knew she was hurting. It was all he could do not to take her into his arms, plead for her forgiveness and insist that they start over. But not here, not now.

"Lorelei, I can explain. I know what I did wasn't right and I do regret it. We need to talk, but this just isn't a good time. I've got major problems here that are going to get worse before they get better."

He took a deep breath, wishing the pain would stop, knowing that it wouldn't. "You can't stay."

She flinched slightly, but otherwise didn't react. Her chin lifted as she met his eyes. Coolly she asked, "What makes you think I want to?"

Lucas hesitated. He didn't really know how to respond. Of course she would be upset at him, she had every right, but if her intention was outright rejection, why had she come? Just to put the knife in? That seemed so completely unlike the woman he thought he knew that he could not credit it.

"All right," he said quietly, "suppose you tell me why you did come?"

Lorelei took a deep breath. She had tried to prepare herself for this, but she wasn't fooling herself. Now that the moment was at hand she was as far from being ready as she possibly could be.

Still, she had come this far. She had no choice but to go the distance.

"I want to know what happened between your family and my father," she said quietly.

Lucas stiffened. He hadn't expected this. "Brandeis *was* well-informed," he said.

"My father's records are chaotic, but I do know for sure that your family was involved in building the house."

"They spent three years of their lives on it," Lucas said. He spoke quietly, almost expressionlessly, but the darkness in his eyes said far more. "My grandfather and his brother devoted almost every waking moment to the house. They took tremendous pride in their work, but they also believed that what they built for your father would lead to other projects further down the line. Their intention was to found a successful construction firm that would enable them to provide for their families in the way they wanted to."

"What went wrong?" Lorelei asked quietly.

"Several things. Unfortunately they had no contract and they were far too trusting. Money they put out for supplies, which they went into debt to get, was never repaid. They ended up bankrupt. But more than that, during the final weeks on the job, my great-uncle was severely injured in a fall from the roof. He died not too long after. My grandfather tried to convince your father to do something to provide for the widow and children, but Vincent McGee refused. He left the family without a penny, reeling from a tragedy and with no hope of the future they had struggled so hard to attain."

Lorelei heard him out in silence. She had no choice. Her throat was too tight for her to make a sound even had she wanted to.

With difficulty, she took a deep breath and murmured, "I see."

"Do you?" Lucas asked gently. "You loved your father. I'm sure you don't want to believe any of this about him."

"I don't," she acknowledged, "but I've seen the records. He turned everything over to business managers who either ignored whatever they were supposed to do or seized the opportunity to rob him blind. I can't prove that, of course, but huge amounts of money just seemed to vanish without Dad even being aware of it. He lived in a world of his own making, and as long as he could stay there, he didn't much care what went on anywhere else."

She spoke matter-of-factly, but Lucas wasn't fooled. Being Vincent McGee's daughter had been a lonely business.

"I'm sorry about what happened," she said softly. "I know that's completely inadequate, but I really mean it and if I could change it, I would."

Lucas's breath caught. He had wronged this woman, using her as he had and leaving with hardly a word. But rather than turn on him in anger, she saw his pain and tried to make amends for it. A fierce sense of protectiveness stirred within him. He was driven to shelter her even from himself.

"Why did you leave when you did?" she asked.

He hesitated. The habit of shouldering sole responsibility was strong within him. But there was no question that he owed her an explanation.

"There's a problem on a development I built here. It's gotten a little nasty. I—"

He broke off as the sudden squeal of tires on the street outside interrupted him. For an instant they both stood there in the living room, frozen by the sound. But only for an instant.

Lucas surged toward her, taking her with his hard body and dragging her to the ground. Lorelei gasped as the breath rushed from her. She was aware of him above her, sheltering her, male strength and warmth enveloping her. But hard on that came shock and fear as the glass in the large picture window suddenly shattered, and she heard a dull thud not far from her head.

Lucas was up first. He reached the broken window in time to see the car pulling away at high speed. It rounded the corner and was out of sight.

Lorelei rose more slowly. She sat on the thick carpeting and stared at the brick, lying not more than a few feet away from her.

"What on earth . . . ?" she began.

Lucas returned to her. He held out a hand, which she instinctively took. At her first glimpse of his face, she flinched. Never in her life had she seen anyone so coldly enraged. His eyes were steel, his mouth taut. Harshly he said, "You have to leave. Now."

Twelve

The Delite Donut Shop was tucked in between a dry cleaner and a bank on the main shopping strip made to resemble a village main street from the previous century. At this hour, late afternoon, the shop was all but empty. A round-faced woman with creamy brown skin poured Lorelei coffee, allowed as to how the cinnamon buns weren't bad and left her to herself.

Lorelei sat by the window, staring out at the street. She stirred her coffee absently, preoccupied with her thoughts. Her parting from Lucas had been swift and painful. His absolute insistence that she leave left no time for anything else. As far as he was concerned, the problem was his own and he would deal with it. Her only function was to go away.

Part of her wanted to just get in the car and head straight back to San Cristobal. But she couldn't do it. Twice before in her life she had been denied the chance to help someone she cared about, first with Tony and then with her father. Both experiences had hurt her more than she wanted to admit, even to herself. She wasn't going to go through that again, not if she could possibly help it.

She stirred restlessly in the seat. As she did so, her eyes fell to the newspaper the previous occupant of the table had left behind. It was the morning's Mountain Falls *Gazette*. The front-page headline read "Investigation Continues Into Charges of Toxic Waste Dumping Near Cluster Housing. Residents Outraged."

The article below continued what was clearly an ongoing story about accusations that illegal dumping had gone on in a nature preserve next to the housing development built by Messina Construction.

Lorelei put the paper down slowly and sat back in her chair. The coffee grew cold as she considered what this could mean for Lucas.

The woman returned to ask if she wanted any-thing more. Lorelei shook her head. Aware that she must look distracted and concerned, she mustered a half smile as she reached for her purse to pay.

As she left the doughnut shop, she noticed several people outside talking earnestly among themselves. Uncertain what to do next, she spied a convenience store and went in.

A radio was on in the store, loud enough for her to hear it. The newscaster was saying, "Word of the possible illegal waste dumping in the vicinity of the Mountain Falls development has raised great con-cern on the part of residents there. An angry group met this morning with builder Lucas Messina, who said that he doubted the reports were true but pledged that he would do everything possible to as-sess the situation. Messina further assured residents that if toxic wastes are present, he will buy back all units that have been sold and shut down the devel-opment. Irate property owners said the situation merited immediate action and accused Messina of risking their safety. And now on the weather..."

Lorelei let her breath out slowly, tuning out the rest of the broadcast. It was even worse than she'd thought. From the sound of it, Lucas was under great pressure to take steps that would destroy his business. Those steps might turn out to be unavoidable, but the situation was far from certain. Meanwhile, he was being threatened by violence that was turning increasingly dangerous and personal. Her stomach churned at the thought of what could happen to him.

A young man emerged from the back of the store. He was tall and slender with a narrow, freckled face and a shy smile.

"Sorry," he said when he saw her, "I didn't realize anyone was there. What can I do for you?"

Lorelei cleared her throat. "The local paper, are their offices around here?"

"Right down the street."

She nodded, still not sure what she meant to do but certain that she absolutely could not leave. Anything was better than that. Maybe she really wouldn't be able to help, but she had to try.

Her mind made up, she got back into the car. Moments later, she drew up in front of the offices of the Mountain Falls *Gazette*.

Lorelei sneezed, again. Not surprising considering the dust she'd been breathing for the last several hours. The nice lady at the front counter hadn't had any qualms about letting her into the *Gazette*'s morgue, not after she explained that she was doing research on the Mountain Falls area.

Nobody thought to ask for more details or even for any identification. They were simply far too busy to bother.

The *Gazette* was a small operation, occupying the lower floor of a three-story building on the main street. There were perhaps a half-dozen employees and they were all run ragged, trying to answer the phones, which rang constantly.

Lorelei had overheard snatches of their conversations as she made her way back toward the morgue. Yes, they had information about toxic waste dumping in the nature preserve. No, they weren't revealing their sources. Yes, they would stay with the story and report anything more they discovered. No, there was nothing to rumors of strange deaths in the development.

Residents were calling from throughout the town and the surrounding area to try to find out what was going on. So were advertisers, who were up in arms at the bad effect the story could have on sales of all sorts. Everybody had a question, an opinion, a fear, an angle.

Everybody wanted answers. Including Lorelei, but she wasn't expecting to get them from the newspaper's employees. They were clearly in over their heads and scrambling frantically.

If there were any answers, she was sure they lay elsewhere, in the dusty back room, for instance, where she was slowly but steadily going through the copies of the *Gazette* published several years before, when the development was first proposed.

Lucas had apparently bought the land in the early 1980s, before the big run-up on prices, but had done nothing with it until several years later, when he presented plans to the town for construction of cluster housing. A series of hearings had been held. Various protests were raised about environmental concerns. There also seemed to have been a faction within the town that wanted to slow down development in general.

Nothing unusual there. The same issues were being dealt with everywhere. From what she could gather, Lucas had been very patient in dealing with the townspeople. He had ordered his own environmental studies, beyond what the law required, and had made all the data available to anyone who wanted to see it.

At the suggestion of a self-appointed committee of residents, various modifications had been made to the project that seemed largely cosmetic, but which had made it more acceptable. By the time construction began, there seemed to be considerable goodwill between Lucas and the residents of Mountain Falls.

And yet... there had also been a series of accidents on the construction site. Several men had been injured. Lucas had even halted work at one point to identify the problem before anything more could happen. He seemed to have managed it, because after that everything had gone smoothly.

Lorelei put away the last copy of the paper—the *Gazette* hadn't yet moved on to microfiche—and shook her head slowly. She had hoped to uncover a motive for someone to want to sabotage the development even at this late stage, but she hadn't managed it.

Going back out past the counter, she noticed that everyone was still busy juggling phones. The concern ignited by the story showed no signs of abating.

It was getting on for late afternoon. Her stomach rumbled. The thought of food had no appeal, but she knew that she had to eat. She found a sandwich shop down the street, placed an order and took it back to the car. Sitting behind the wheel, she could still see the entrance to the *Gazette*.

Her sandwich was almost finished when she glanced absently at the man coming out of the building. She hadn't noticed him inside, and she suspected she would have. He was tall and slender,

with a rangy build, unkempt brown hair and a nose
that looked as though it had been broken at least
once. Dressed in old jeans, a work shirt and what
looked like an army surplus jacket, he moved with
nervous speed down the block until he was out of
sight.

Lorelei stared after him. There was something
about him . . .

She put the sandwich aside, dug in her purse and
found the small sketch pad. Quickly, before she
could think about what she was doing, she drew the
man's face. She had only seen him for a few moments, so the sketch was necessarily rough. But when
she looked it over, her suspicion was confirmed—he
was definitely familiar.

Moreover, she knew where she had seen him before. Her hand shook slightly as she gunned the motor and pulled away from the curb.

Thirteen

Lucas parked the Cord in front of the house and walked swiftly up the steps to the front door. He pressed the bell, listening to it chime hollowly deep within.

Minutes passed without a response. He rang again, waiting, until impatience got the better of him. He tried the doorknob, finding it securely locked. Going back down the steps, he walked around the house. All the windows were closed. There was no sign of any activity inside.

Or outside, either. By the side driveway, he stopped. Lorelei's car was gone.

She was in town, he told himself. Shopping, most likely. She'd be back in a few minutes. He'd wait.

He wandered down toward the gazebo and, on impulse, went inside. It was a pretty place, secluded and romantic. He smiled faintly as he remembered the one time he'd been in it before.

But the smile faded quickly as he glanced again toward the house. Where was she?

He forced himself to sit down on the bench. From the pocket of his jacket, he withdrew Lorelei's small sketch pad. Slowly he opened it and looked at the face she had drawn.

Left on his own, he would never have thought of Hal Davies. The man had worked for him less than three months during construction of the Mountain Falls project. He'd been fired after a series of accidents was tied to his carelessness.

Lucas's mouth tightened as he remembered his swift response to the mishaps that had suddenly plagued the development. His great-uncle's death had sensitized him to the danger that threatened any construction job. He had promised himself long ago that no man would be injured through his own greed or unconcern.

As a result, Messina Construction had an outstanding safety record. When the accidents had started at Mountain Falls, Lucas had gone himself to investigate. It took him several weeks, but eventually he discovered that each accident was the result of a mistake made by one man, Hal Davies.

He told Davies in no unmistakable terms what he thought of work so shoddy that it looked as though it was deliberately intended to harm. There had been no way to prove that, of course, but he'd wasted no time in firing the man. That was the last he'd seen of him until he'd run him to ground a few days before, at a trailer park outside of town.

Lorelei's note, still attached to the pad, was short and to the point.

Do you know this man? He's in a photo the *Gazette* ran of the development when it was beginning construction and he was in to see someone at the paper today.

Nothing more. He'd found the pad on his doorstep when he'd returned from yet another meeting with the residents. It had taken him an hour or so to put a name to the face, another day to find Hal Davies and convince him that what he wanted most in life was to relocate to an entirely different part of the country, where he would spend his remaining years fervently hoping never to encounter Lucas Messina again. But first, before he could do that, he had a call to pay with Lucas at the offices of the *Gazette*.

Having their source recant sincerely, vigorously and at great length—until finally even Lucas had told him that he'd said enough—had a remarkable effect on the newspaper's staff. The front-page retraction said it all. They had been misled, the so-called proof of toxic waste dumping had been provided by a disgruntled employee who had fabricated the whole affair. The editors formally apologized to Messina Construction—anything to avoid legal action—and assured the residents of the development that they could not possibly be safer.

Everyone breathed a collective sigh of relief—except Davies, who'd wasted no time in making himself scarce.

Problem solved, crisis settled, and with units selling faster than ever thanks—in a weird sort of way—to all the publicity, Lucas was free to return to San Cristobal. The Cord had a top speed of slightly over a hundred miles an hour. He was much too responsible a person to drive it that fast on a public highway. But he had come close.

Much good that it did him. He waited another hour before resigning himself to the fact that Lorelei wasn't going to show up anytime soon. Reluctantly he headed for the office.

* * *

Lisa had the usual stack of work awaiting his attention. She ran down the list of messages, memos, people who needed to see him and so on until she realized he was barely listening.

"Something wrong?" she asked softly, looking at the tall, powerfully built man who stood at the windows of his office, his shoulders tight and an ineffable air of tension surrounding him.

Quietly he said, "I don't know."

His answer surprised her, she was so used to her boss always being in command, always being decisive, always being absolutely certain about what he wanted and how he was going to get it. This—whatever this was—was different.

"Do me a favor?" he asked.

"Sure," Lisa said hastily.

He bent over his desk and scribbled a number. "Call this until you get an answer, then let me know."

Lisa glanced at the number. It was local, somewhere in San Cristobal. "Okay. Should I ask for anyone in particular?"

"Lorelei McGee."

Her eyebrows rose slightly. "Vincent McGee's daughter?"

"That's the one."

"I heard she'd come back for the funeral and stayed on."

"You haven't seen her in the last few days, have you?"

The sudden urgency in his voice roused Lisa's interest even more. She shook her head regretfully. "I've never seen her. You...uh...know each other?"

He nodded once. "Let me know if you get through to her."

Lisa assured him she would and returned to her desk. She tried the number at once but without result. Five minutes later she tried it again. Throughout the remainder of the day, she continued to press the automatic redial button at regular intervals. She lost count of how many times she called the number, but there was never an answer.

"I'm sorry," she said when she went in to report before leaving for the day. "She isn't home and there's no answering machine."

"She's got to be somewhere," Lucas said, almost to himself. He sounded worried. Lisa hated to leave him under such circumstances, but it was clear that he wanted to be alone. Still, she was glad when she ran into Sal on her way out. Ordinarily she would never have mentioned anything her boss was doing, even to one of his relatives, but this time she made an exception.

Sal stuck his head in the door of Lucas's office and frowned at what he saw. His cousin was slumped in the chair behind his worktable. He didn't look anything at all like a man who had just defused a disaster in the making. On the contrary, he looked like just about nothing in his life was going right.

"How's it going?" Sal asked as he sauntered in and casually took a seat on the other side of the table.

Lucas raised an eyebrow and glanced at him discouragingly. "Lousy."

Sal was taken aback. This was his cousin, the head of their family, the man they all looked up to? What could possibly have happened to bring about such a change in him?

"Hey," he said softly, "let's get a drink, okay? Marie won't mind if I'm home late today, and you look like you could use a little morale boost."

Lucas would have preferred to stay right where he was, brooding over Lorelei. But he realized Sal had a point. Slowly he stood up and reached for his jacket.

Sherree's was open, but the crowd had yet to arrive. They took a table toward the back and ordered a round of beers. The mugs were half-empty before Sal spoke.

"So what's the deal? I've never seen you like this before."

"I've never done anything this stupid before," Lucas said. He laughed faintly when he saw the look on Sal's face. "Don't worry, it's got nothing to do with business."

"Who said it did? I know you too well to think that. This has to be personal."

Sal took another swallow of his beer and looked at his cousin over the rim of the glass. "So who is she?"

Lucas's eyebrows rose. "She?"

"Hey, it had to happen eventually. I'll tell you what, I'll take a guess. If I get it right, you own up. Deal?"

Lucas didn't answer directly, he merely shrugged.

"Lorelei McGee."

Sal had the satisfaction of seeing his cousin caught off guard. Ruefully, Lucas asked, "Is it that obvious?"

"You were hung up on the house. Now you're hung up on the woman. These things happen."

"It isn't quite the same," Lucas said.

"How come?"

"It just isn't." Not for the world would he admit to Sal that he could live without the house—easily. Lorelei was another story altogether.

"What went wrong?"

"Nothing much," Lucas said sardonically. "I lied to her, deliberately misled her about my intentions, concealed my true identity and then went off with hardly a word, leaving her to find out for herself who I was and what I was up to. Pretty smart."

Sal whistled softly. "This doesn't sound like you."

"Doesn't feel like me, either," Lucas admitted. "But that's what happened and now there's no sign of her. Lisa tried to reach the house all day, with no luck."

"Maybe she was just busy somewhere. Whatta you say we take a ride out there right now?"

Lucas appreciated the gesture, but he shook his head. "I'll try her again later. If she still doesn't answer, I'm not sure what I'll do."

"There's gotta be somebody who knows where she went. Does she have any friends around here?"

"She never mentioned any. I got the impression being Vincent McGee's daughter wasn't exactly a bed of roses. She grew up kind of isolated."

"Okay, but there should be people he knew, in the same line of work. There was a big turnout for his funeral, wasn't there?"

Lucas thought about that. Sal had a point. There had been a crowd at the cemetery and after that, at the house, he'd had that run-in with the tough old dame... what was her name?

"Here," Sherree said as she stuck a plate of nachos under his nose. "You don't look good. Eat something."

Lucas ignored the food and stared at her. "Sherree, how old are you?"

Sal choked on his beer, grabbing for a napkin.

"I take it back," Sherree said, reaching for the nachos. "You don't need food. You need a doctor."

"I'm sorry," Lucas said unrepentantly, "let me put that differently. It's my impression that you are a lady of wisdom and experience. Am I wrong?"

Sherree put a hand on her hip, tossed her head and awarded him a tiny smile. "Well, if you're going to put it that way, no, you aren't wrong."

"I could use some help. Recently I met a woman of—shall we say—a certain age. I can't place her, but I think you might be able to."

"In what context?" Sherree asked.

"Show business, the movies, a friend of Vincent McGee's."

She nodded slowly. "Okay, shoot, what did she look like?"

Lucas told her. He didn't get very far before she gave him a chiding look. "What's the world coming to? You honestly don't know who Melinda Taylor is?"

"The name's familiar," Lucas admitted. "But—"

"But nothing. That's who you met. I can't believe you didn't recognize her. Don't you ever watch television? Her movies are on all the time."

"Probably after my bedtime," Lucas murmured.

"She was an incredible star," Sherree went on. She had a fond smile on her face, as though recollecting her own youth. "One of the most beautiful women ever, the kind who lit up the screen. She was also a very dear friend of Vincent McGee's."

"She was at the house after the funeral," Lucas said.

"Of course, she would have been. I'd love a chance to meet her. I always wondered why she and Thad Morley never got married. They were meant for each other."

"You wouldn't have any idea where I might be able to reach her, would you?" Lucas asked.

Sherree thought for a moment. "I seem to remember she had an incredible house in Beverly Hills, bought it before the place became so fashionable. I wouldn't be surprised if she still lives there."

Lucas excused himself. He walked into the vestibule where the pay phone was located. The information operator couldn't have been more helpful.

M. Taylor on Palisades Drive in Beverly Hills had a listed phone number. The operator was happy to share it.

Fourteen

The cabin was at the end of a dirt road that wound past a small, pristine lake. Lucas passed the turnoff for it twice before he finally got it right.

Melly's directions—she had bid him call her by her nickname in a burst of rare familiarity occasioned by the discovery of his intentions toward Lorelei—were less than precise. But her heart was in the right place. Otherwise, as she was at pains to tell him, she would never have revealed "Dear Lorelei's" special place.

It was special, Lucas thought as he stopped the car and got out. The cabin was surrounded by tall, stately pines that scented the air. The building itself was completely unpretentious, made of rough-hewn logs fitted together in the time-honored fashion. There were gingham curtains at the windows. A curl of smoke rose from the chimney.

For the first time in too long, Lucas felt the tension easing from him. All during the ride up, he had worried over what Lorelei would say when she saw him. More often than he wanted to remember, he had glanced at the sketch pad on the seat beside him. Hal Davies's picture was gone, turned over to the authorities in Mountain Falls in case he was ever foolish enough to return. But the sketches Lorelei had made on the headland were still there, including the portrait of him.

He had actually blushed the first time he saw it. There was no doubting that it was him, she hadn't actually embellished his appearance. But there was a feeling to the sketch, an emotion embedded in it that gave him enormous hope.

He paused, hands deep in his pockets, and surveyed the cabin. The smoke indicated someone was at home. He had thought about calling, but decided against it. Now he hesitated only briefly before striding decisively toward the front door.

It opened before he could knock. He forgot whatever it was he had planned to say, something witty and erudite, no doubt, and simply stared. Lorelei was wearing a dress. He'd never actually seen her in one before. It wasn't a fancy dress, just some kind of pretty cotton print in rose and lavender, buttoned down the front. Her hair hung loose around her shoulders. There were shadows under her eyes, he couldn't help but notice them, but they didn't change anything. She looked like everything he had ever dreamed of in his life all rolled up into one delightful, exquisite, infinitely desirable package.

"Hi," he said. It came out more like a growl than a word, so he cleared his throat and tried again. "Hi."

She smiled. Not a little smile, not a slight one, but a full-blown, hold-nothing-back, knock-your-eyes-out smile, as if seeing him standing there on her doorstep was the best thing that had ever happened to her in her life. Also, possibly the most remarkable.

"Hi," she said.

They stood there, staring at each other for a long moment, before they both laughed self-consciously.

"I happened to be in the neighborhood," Lucas began.

"There is no neighborhood," Lorelei pointed out, not unreasonably. "This is the original back-of-beyond."

"So Melly told me."

Her eyebrows shot up. *"Melly?* She lets you call her Melly? I had to know her eighteen years before I was granted that privilege and then it had to be *Aunt* Melly."

"I'm too old for that. We're strictly first name basis."

"I'm impressed," Lorelei said. She stepped aside. "Come on in."

Lucas didn't need to be asked twice. The main room of the cabin was bigger than he would have expected from the outside. It had a high ceiling crossed by rough-hewn beams, a fieldstone fireplace that took up most of one wall, and a scattering of good but obviously comfortable furniture. There was a drawing board set up near a window. It looked as though she had been working, or at least trying to.

"I was coming back," she said quickly. "I just needed a little time away to think things over."

He nodded, hoping the full extent of his relief didn't show. After the stunt he'd pulled, he couldn't have blamed her if she'd simply opted out on him. Not that he would have accepted that. On the contrary, he would have moved heaven and earth to find her.

As it was, all he'd had to do was convince one aged but still sharp-as-a-tack movie star that his heart was in the right place.

"How did you and Melly happen to get acquainted?" Lorelei asked.

"I called her to ask if she knew where you were."

"And she told you, just like that?"

"Well, no, not exactly. First I had to do a little convincing."

Lorelei's mouth twitched at the corners. She could still hardly believe that he was standing there in her living room, looking solid, strong and so blessedly real. Just as she'd been wishing for in the days since she returned from San Cristobal, the yearning growing with each passing moment, even as she tried to convince herself to be sensible, get a grip on herself, not hope for too much. All that tiresomely reasonable stuff she was just no good at.

"Are you hungry?" she asked. It seemed an appropriate question. He'd had a long drive.

Lucas met her eyes, his gaze silvered with raw, frank need. "Yes."

She flushed, feeling the heat stain her cheeks. "I meant..."

"I know what you meant." He took a step toward her, unable any longer to bear the distance between them. Quietly he said, "I'm sorry."

A soft sigh escaped her. "So am I."

His brow creased. "You have nothing to be sorry for."

"I'm sorry you went through what you did, that your whole family suffered. It wasn't right."

"It was a long time ago."

"You didn't feel that way when you came to the house." Quickly, before he could interrupt, she went on, "I said I came up here to do some thinking. I've decided that it would be foolish of me to keep such a big place. If you want it, it's yours."

He stared at her. "Just like that?"

She nodded. "Just like that." Firmly she added, "The men in your family built it to last, but someone needs to take better care of it than I can afford to do. I make a good living, but not enough for that. You'd really be doing me a favor by taking it off my hands."

"I thought you loved the place," he said gently.

"To tell you the truth, since I've had a chance to think things over, I have mixed feelings about it. The smartest decision I made was to get away after Tony died. I came up here, made a place of my own and found the work that was right for me. I missed my father and his friends, but for the first time in my life, I was a fully functioning adult. I'd never want to go backward on that."

"I'd never want you to, either," he said. He reached out and very gently took hold of her. "You're a beautiful woman, Lorelei McGee, inside and out. You're kind, generous, passionate and forgiving. From where I stand, that beats stone and mortar any day.''

A light kindled in her eyes, but a cautious one. "We haven't really known each other that long."

"That's what Melly said."

"Oh? And what did you tell her?"

"That I was looking forward to spending the rest of my life getting very, very well acquainted with you."

A soft laugh escaped her, born of hope cracking out of its shell, fluffing up its wings, getting ready to soar.

"She must have loved that."

"Sure seemed to. Who's Thad, by the way?"

"An honorary uncle. Why?"

"Melly said he'd want to be the one to give you away."

Lorelei sniffed. Her heart started doing a rat-a-tat against her ribs, so loudly that she was sure he could hear. "It sounds as though you and she had a nice, long talk."

"Under five minutes. I was in a hurry."

She tilted her head back and met his gaze. The silver had turned molten. Her breath caught as warmth curled through her. "You still are."

His laughter was low, intimate, infinitely male. It unleashed liquid heat deep within her. "Give me half a chance," he said, "and I'll show you how patient I can be."

She pretended to think about it. "Exactly how long do you think this demonstration will take?"

Lucas bent slightly, lifting her in his arms. "Fifty, sixty years, maybe more."

"Hmm, I don't know," she murmured, a little breathlessly. He was carrying her toward the short flight of steps that led to the loft bedroom, and she couldn't for the life of her think of any reason why he should stop. "Sounds like a long time."

"It is," Lucas agreed. He stopped on the bottom step and smiled down at her. "I'll tell you what, how about you give me until morning to convince you? That's fair."

Her eyes widened slightly. "Morning? You think you can do it by then?"

His smile deepened, reaching right through her. "I can sure try."

Much later, closer to afternoon than morning, Lorelei stirred. She lifted herself up on her elbows and regarded Lucas bemusedly. He was fast asleep, as well he ought to be.

The sun had fled behind clouds. A soft, silken rain fell through the pine trees. She pulled the covers more snugly over them both and stretched out beside him.

Her eyes drifted shut. Behind them, images danced of the house on the cliff above the ocean, no longer empty but alive with love and laughter, the sounds of children and the promise of joy found so unexpectedly somewhere between a dream and reality.

* * * * *